GW00692185

The Gatestrian Knights

R.J. Godlewski

Fultus™ Books

The Gatestrian Knights

by

R.J. Godlewski

ISBN 1-59682-064-0

Copyright © 2005 by Ronald John Godlewski
All rights reserved.

Published by Fultus Corporation

Corporate Web Site: http://www.fultus.com
Fultus eLibrary: http://elibrary.fultus.com
Online Book Superstore: http://store.fultus.com
Writer Web Site http://writers.fultus.com/godlewski/

No part of this book may be used or reproduced in any manner whatsoever without written permission except
in the case of brief quotations embodied in reviews and critical articles.
This is the work of fiction.
Names, characters, places, and incidents are the product of the author's imagination or are used fictitiously
and any resemblance to actual persons living or dead, events or locales, is entirely coincidental.
The author and publisher have made every effort in the preparation of this book to ensure the accuracy of the
information. However, the information contained in this book is offered without warranty, either express or
implied. Neither the author nor the publisher nor any dealer or distributor will be held liable for any
damages caused or alleged to be caused either directly or indirectly by this book.

In loving memory of my precious Sara
(07/25/51 —12/13/03)
who always encouraged me
right up until the last.

In love with you,
ALWAYS!!!

1

JASON TASK LONGED for the seclusion and sanctity of his northeastern Wyoming spread, the ten thousand acre ranch that served as his personal retreat from the masses that seemed hell-bent on driving him mad. He had nothing personal against people; he just viewed them with the same quiet indifference that he showed the herd of bison that grazed on the property, perhaps a little less.

His need to adapt to global business and his desire for personal freedom created something of a dual personality within his psyche. One, the astute, cultured businessman whose holdings circled the planet, and the other, the quiet, opinionated rancher whose quest for seclusion was served equally by the Jagged T Ranch and countless expeditions into the Pacific waters.

Jason made friends easily and frequently, yet the same was also true for his enemies, many of whom devoted their existence to his demise. His was a simple take on life; either you were right or wrong, and therefore either good or evil. No gray area was permitted.

This might've proven to be a problem had he created a retail or entertainment enterprise, but Tactical Extractions, Ltd. was neither. Jason Task provided that one most valuable of all commodities: *Freedom*. If one were held captive, lost within a hostile territory, or otherwise denied basic human rights, Tactical Extractions could rescue you — an invaluable option in a rapidly threatening world.

Aside from the romantic nature of the profession, Jason's business dealings were fairly straightforward. Indeed, he shared much in common with the dozens of overnight delivery agencies that spanned the globe, the primary logistical difference being that he dealt with human lives. Still, ninety percent of his efforts were no more strenuous than the acquisition of airline tickets and hotel reservations often flared with ten percent that involved major military action and delicate domestic diplomacy.

Jason knew that he was right, if somewhat hated. Life was precious. Innocent life more so. His wealth did not come by way of social privilege and he took advantage of every opportunity to distribute his fortune and talents to those who needed it the most. Yet, he was highly selective in both his philanthropy and his consultations. One didn't become one of the richest individuals in the world by being a fool.

International extractions of the human kind required tact, discipline, well financed resources, and friends permanently anchored in high places. Jason Task had all of these qualities and more. He was intelligent, resourceful, and very determined. His crystalline definition of right and wrong often bordered upon the hypocritical, but he danced along the line with the grace and determination of an expert. People who were in trouble and needed his company's services mattered, semantics did not.

Jason's beliefs were forged partly by religious conviction – he attended Mass weekly and frequently prayed the rosary – and partly by narcissism – if God was going to punish him, then it would be for what *he* did and not because of what others forced him to do. Regardless of their origin, his beliefs were sincere and firm. They had to be.

Given the nature of Tactical Extractions, much had to be achieved in secrecy. Entering hostile territory with the intent of removing hostages or dissidents could not be done out in the open. Hence, Jason Task owned many businesses in such fields as computer technology, agriculture, commercial fishing, air transportation, and construction to name a few. He required the ability to be in all places at all times with the equipment necessary to accomplish a host of tasks, and all had to be done as legally as possible.

Nicknamed "Hazardous Task" by his best friend and business' number two, Jack Stephens, Jason took on a mystique that was hard to squash. Political figures feared him, despots despised him, and military commanders did not trust him. To the general public he was a hero; to the general administration he was a villain.

Any activity of this nature was destined to be defined as purely mercenary in nature and any proponent as simply a Soldier of Fortune. Jason Task, however, was neither a Whore of War nor an adventurer. He was a businessman with a passion for the underdog.

Such activities did not lead towards an easy life. Samantha, his wife, died of throat cancer many years earlier, her presence oblivious to the achievements that he would accomplish later on. He did not remarry, or even date. He could not bear to replace her with someone who more likely than not would turn out to be inferior in his eyes. Nor would it be fair for someone else to constantly battle with her memory. So, for the most part, he diverted his attention to creating things – businesses, organizations, forms of art, etc. In her memory, he did everything. In her absence, he questioned even that.

Time might've healed all wounds for others, but it always sat eager, lost somewhere in the back of his consciousness until it reared its ugly head and hastened any activity in which he was involved. Constantly he second guessed the treatment that Samantha received, wondering whether this or that would've prolonged her life. He became obsessed with wealth. Not the materialism of the New Age world, but pure monetary subsistence.

"If I had money then," he would always be overheard as saying, "then just maybe Sam would be alive today." It was a useless argument and he knew it, but it showed the world that he wouldn't let others go through what he had gone through.

Tactical Extractions was a natural evolution of this belief. By amassing wealth and equipment, he could ensure that the unfortunate would be served by his company and his personal philosophies. For him, the people of the world didn't need another charitable organization. They needed their own security force, independent of nations and administrations.

Greatness throughout history, he knew, was manifested by individuals, not committees. The Pyramids, the Suez Canal, the Panama Canal – all achievements largely ensured by the superhuman endurance and motivation of a single individual. Jason's empire was one inspired by dedication towards the preservation of individual lives, a reoccurring theme resulting from the loss of his beloved Samantha, the event that changed his life unlike any other.

Prior to her death, Jason was a typical forty year old man, living out a normal life largely unknown to the rest of the world. Samantha had been twelve years his senior and more than just a wife. She was his best friend, confidant, and his entire existence. She represented everything good about his character.

When Sam passed away, she took this goodness away from him and all that remained was a cynical, somewhat confused individual who doubted everything that he once held dear. True, these were the normal thoughts of anyone who had witnessed the virtual destruction of a loved one, but something else also happened to his character.

Jason's emotions waned. He was simply worn away from caring for his beloved wife. In short, he had no *feelings* left. On the one hand, he was glad that she was no longer suffering and had many visions of her appearance in Heaven during his sleep. This made him happy, for he knew that if anyone was in Heaven, it was her.

On the other hand, however, he had *felt* her passing. He felt the evil part of her, as minimal as it was, being ripped away from her soul so that she could enter Paradise direct. These evil spirits, he believed, tormented him for several weeks following her death. His character suffered, allowing him to become more cynical, more demanding, and relinquishing any undue emotional concern towards those closest to him.

For the most part, he was the same person that he'd always been. The primary difference now was the destruction of the *naiveté* that epitomized his life before he realized that truly horrible things can happen to *anyone*. Gone was the denial phase; life was indeed tough.

Samantha hadn't been part of his life; she had been his whole life. Now she was gone and he had turned his attention towards business and became successful. Though she could no longer participate within his life directly, he made no reservations as to why he was successful now. His life still held a purpose, and it was she who gave him this motivation.

Although she was physically gone, spiritually she was with him and time, even more than a decade of it, did little to quell her influence as Jason was constantly reminded of his beloved Samantha. Her favorite color or movie or song frequently made an appearance and quickly darted past his stoic consciousness and memories of their life together flowed freely.

Jason often wondered why he handled her death so well when compared with others who had attempted suicide or loss faith in God and in life. Quietly, he assumed that it was because of the length of her illness; he had been worn down so deeply that when the time finally came, he was simply exhausted and could no longer fight off the inevitable.

Her dignity in handling her own death also played no small role in his admiration for his wife. She remained concerned for others right up until the moment that she passed away. She had appeared most beautiful as she laid in a coma, her facial deformations seemingly erased as she passed from one life into the other. For her husband, it wasn't so gradual.

One moment, she lay as beautiful as an angel. The next, a greenish corpse devoid of any similarity to Samantha lay in her place. The emotions for Jason ranged from fear to anger to frustration to relief to numbness in such intensity and complexity as he never imagined before, and within the timeframe of only a few seconds in duration. It was during this instantaneous moment of life altering events that Jason realized that his wife had won the battle over the evil spirits that try to control all humans.

The intervening years had educated him, but the memory of that day was as clear as could be. He was now, in all reality, a half person, desperately longing for her presence and equally determined never to forget her influence upon his life. She had made him what he was to become, but she did not have enough time to finish her assignment, and he feared that he would return to his pre-Samantha personality.

Prior to meeting Sam by way of a chance meeting at a local factory, Jason was something of a recluse, fairly uneducated as to the practicalities of life. He had experience, but failed to practice common sense. He strove for business success, but failed to realize that most people, especially those whom he was trying to emulate, did not share his confidence and enthusiasm.

Most people, regardless of place or time of birth, do not have major expectations. They've become accustomed to notions of longevity at jobs, struggling to place food on the table, and never having a say in matters that matter most to them. Jason had almost a child-like belief in anything being possible. He had much to learn.

The youthful Task believed that all he had to do was have an idea and sooner or later, things would work out in his favor. This led him to such disasters as having signed contracts for real estate investments without having the wherewithal to finance the deal and once being sued for hundreds of thousands of dollars for promoting an expedition to the Amazon in order to engage as a wildlife photographer.

Samantha had changed all of this, and firmly grounded his dreams to the earth. His experiences with her engaged him with thoughts that hard work was, well, *hard*. He learned that dreams were fine and that having a great woman behind him made everything seem possible, but that reality dictated a certain price that remained to be paid. Often, they had to go without food or material possessions, struggling to make payments and more than once being evicted because employment opportunities were few and far between.

In the years since her death, his new rationalization of life kept his ambitions at bay, but even this could not bury them completely. Rather, his shattered character gave him just enough cynicism and solitude to slowly work towards his business. He no longer desired either fame or fortune, merely preferring capital success as a means for funding research organizations engaged in pharmaceutical development, for example.

As with many things in life, it was when he gave up the dreams for success that success found him. From designing technology to investing in commercial real estate to creating a shipping company to the final triumph of his aerospace company, his life began to surge forward and it was her presence in Heaven – his very own personal saint – that he knew was the reason for his new blessings.

With the surging capital and more advanced technology provided by his stable of companies, Jason launched Tactical Extractions and the service company quickly became his darling, a tool for which he could alleviate the ills of the world. It was also a business that fit in neatly with his post-Samantha mentality.

What made Tactical Extractions fit in so well with his personality was that he, since his wife's death, became somewhat at odds with the rest of the world. He no longer valued much authority; *he* became his own authority. He once quipped that he listened to only God and the Pope.

A darker, more sinister feeling lay amongst his emotions, one that he rarely thought about. Jason felt that he, alone, was not worthy of the heavenly paradise that his own wife had undoubtedly achieved. It was turmoil between a desire to be with his wife for eternity and a fear that if he, such as he was, was permitted access to the blessed then, somehow, it would reduce the value of the paradise that she existed in.

He never knew if this strange thought subconsciously directed his actions, but he did notice that his desire to do well for the world, largely in memory of Samantha, became something of an obsession for him. When Tactical Extractions took off, he turned philanthropy into a science – a *military* science.

With his newly formed resistance towards authority, Jason Task developed a personal military force to aid those in danger. It was a quirky symbiosis that established a direct link between force and compassion, something that truly matched the current attitudes of its creator. He knew that the primary problem in the world was not famine or disease or even totalitarian rule. It was the inability to get aid to those most in need.

While the so-called United Nations failed in every attempt to be just that – united – and the American political system remained torn between liberal activism and conservative righteousness, Jason Task decided to throw caution into the wind and do what everyone else wanted to do but couldn't. He took matters into his own hands.

Tactical Extractions began simply as a logistics service and grew into the world's foremost paramilitary force, albeit in complete secrecy. Rumors flourished as to what the company's founder was up to, considering that the company that occupied most of his time was by far his smallest enterprise.

Such criticism, however, was quickly dispatched with the plausible explanation that more effort was required to manage the newest and smallest company whereas its larger affiliates were already well established. Only Jason knew that Tactical Extractions was actually the largest of his business enterprises, owning, through various domestic and offshore entities, a sizeable portion of his other companies.

On paper, it looked as though that Jason Task owned a large percentage of several major corporations with various other organizations owning substantial chunks of his businesses. In reality, however, Jason owned everything. With the greater scrutiny afforded to public companies, for example, this ruse may not have been as effective as it was, but for a private company, who owned what wasn't quite as important. Still, the rumors persisted and Jason never quite fought off the charges.

He combined truth with cover stories and made the situation so complicated that not even the best and brightest on Wall Street knew precisely what was fact and what was fiction. The true target of this disinformation scheme, however, was the general public, that massive curtain of stupidity that politicians and strongmen feared.

A single, well orchestrated story, properly timed, could cause so much commotion amongst a country's population as to deflect all but the most arduous investigation. This was even more pronounced if the story in question sided with the public, such as when Task coordinated the story about a third world dictator siphoning off his nation's food supply. The story was hardly news, and even less of a lie, but the results were impressive and nearly toppled the dictator.

Jason had the story placed so that he could send *real* food supplies to a famished village. What nobody realized, however, was that the supplies that the government 'released' were, in fact, the food supplies that Jason wanted to get past a corrupt official. By having the local government accept responsibility for the deliveries, even though they never knew that it wasn't their food, he managed to feed three whole villages without having to resort to bribes or military action.

Sadly, not all of his efforts were as calm. Once, it required a commando team of no less than ninety men to storm an African compound and annihilate the defenders in order to rescue some thirty nuns that were being raped and murdered by the thugs. When religious personnel were being harmed, regardless of their faith or religion, Jason had standing orders to pull out all of the stops. It was one of 'Jason's Rules' and his staff always kept his word.

Maintaining a private army was, at times, bewildering, especially for a tormented individual such as Jason Task and he lost much sleep over his activities. They became his obsession, his passion. He fancied himself a savior of the world and longed for some recognition of the services that he provided incognito. If it weren't for his loyal staff, he figured, he would've vaporized the planet long before.

Jack Stephens, as Jason's number one associate, was just the sort of person who could tame his activities. Cousins through marriage, Jack was himself a successful businessman, owning Stephens Oceanographic, the large Southeastern diving and salvage concern.

Jack's experience in business, his loyalty to family, and his intelligence – he held degrees in oceanography and astrophysics – supported Tactical Extractions' operations well. He also knew something about paramilitary operations, having worked the wars as a younger man, and married into the McIntyre Pharmaceuticals empire, which his wife Jamie took over after her father caused chaos by preventing lifesaving medicines from reaching market.

This combination of trust, intelligence, and business expertise reduced a significant amount of stress from the mind of Jason Task, and more often than not eliminated scrutiny from various parties by allowing the more personable Jack Stephens to work his way into the limelight. Then, whenever matters took a disastrous turn, the amiable Mrs. Stephens would walk in and charm the belligerents.

The Task-Stephens team worked to perfection, cooperating on numerous missions to save people from all over the planet. In fact, it was Jack's notion to turn Tactical Extractions into a salvation service, saving people from all forms of harm and captivity. Not quite as idealistic as his older cousin, Jack was nevertheless very keen on his suspicions that public officials were, as he put it, totally useless in any activity that didn't warrant kissing a baby.

The addition of affiliates in marine logistics and pharmaceutical research completed the global hold of Tactical Extractions, and there was no place on earth that Jason could not justify a presence in. In intelligence gathering alone, this capability improved their chances of success, indeed becoming the sole determining factor on many occasions.

Age, however, tempers even the most inflammatory individual and Jason was no exception to the rule. His longing for peace and tranquility played heavily on his mind for the past several years and he wanted to make an adjustment. Saving the world from itself was all fine and good, but maintaining the status quo was both time consuming and ineffective.

No, he reasoned, he had to change the *systems* in place. He had to ensure that every individual conceived had a fair chance at survival and, this was most important, success. To feed, protect, and educate was fine and dandy, but what chance did humanity have if evil could destroy these individuals after they were nourished, clothed, and taught?

Jason tried desperately to change the equation through numerous contributions to the Catholic Church and its global organizations, but even the Faith lacked the means necessary to defend those most in harm. To "turn the other cheek" was not something that either Jason or Jack cared to do. Therefore, something was needed to bridge the gap between the filial trust of Faith and the convincing power of a strong military force.

To be able to distribute food and medical supplies to an impoverished nation was one thing, to take over that impoverished nation in order to ensure that it could join the league of the civilized world was something altogether different and warranted much debate. Jason knew keenly that such activities would propel him from the thrones of heroism and land him squarely into the fiery pit of damnation.

Inasmuch as many within the world applauded his covert attempts to bring aid to the unfortunate, few would support open hostility and nation tampering. The thought reeked of the very totalitarianism that he had spent the past decade fighting against. No, if his latest mission was to succeed, he would have to bury his activities further into the secret nature of clandestine operations.

Another problem involved Jack's attitude towards this ambition. His younger cousin was more passive than he, and anything that might bring his beautiful wife into harm's way would sever his ties with Jason. Whether Jack would become involved or not, definitely decided whether this larger plan would succeed.

JASON WALKED OVER to his desk that sat conspicuously in the middle of his thirtieth floor office and gazed out through the windows towards the Oklahoma City skyline. He examined each glowing structure intuitively, and thought about the ramifications of his actions.

He was a long way from the seclusion of his Wyoming ranch and the approaching night illuminated the buildings in the distance, enforcing upon him the realization that people were involved, not just despots and terrorists. Everything that he did involved everyday people. To tamper with nations would undoubtedly alter the course of history and what the final outcome would be was up for grabs, regardless of his personal confidence.

Today, the interior lights shone forth from the buildings. Tomorrow, buildings all around the world may begin to blaze forth with real fires, if he were not careful. History would be made for certain, but what history would make of his involvement was equally important.

He reached over and subconsciously fumbled with the rosary that sat on the corner of the desk and mumbled a quiet prayer to Samantha, asking for guidance and, far more important, a simple sign. He believed that Jesus and the saints were in Heaven, but he *knew* that she was; she came to him within many dreams that were far too realistic to be anything but true visions. Because of this, he frequently prayed directly to her, for she was someone that he had actually known and touched, not some abstract saint from centuries past.

Jason had keen faith, but Samantha was his salvation. To receive word from her, regardless of how it was delivered, would ease his mind against reoccurring thoughts that he was somehow venturing into dementia. In all of the years, however, he never knew whether anything that happened ever came from his beloved Sam, yet he kept asking her for her intervention.

Finally releasing the rosary until its beads hit the desk with a soft clink, Jason folded his arms across his chest, leaned back against the wooden desk, and lost himself in thought over the rapidly darkening horizon. Darkness was indeed approaching fast.

The salmon sky hinged itself upon a deep red band that bled from the point where the sun had plunged beneath the horizon and led to a silvery cloak of clouds that metamorphosed into a sea of stars, punctuated by an early meteor arching its ribbon-like path over the planet Venus. Was this apparition a sign from Samantha?

He smiled at the implications. Either his wife was sending him a message that all was going to be okay, or that his ambitions were going to sink with the rapidity of the heavenly visitor that had just ended its trail into a sea of blood red. If this was, in fact, an answer to his prayer, he was no more aware of its interpretation than if he had never had a reply.

"Sam." he spoke loudly, though no one was around to hear. "You always did have a sense of humor."

Jason reached over to the windows and began to close the blinds as the last semblance of twilight vanished beneath the distant horizon, interspersed with tall structures of artificial light. Soon, the only thing that appeared in the windows was his reflection in the glass. He examined the image, ill at ease over the signs of age becoming more evident within the features of his face.

Attitude had a lot to do with age and Jason was no different than anyone else. He always envisioned himself as being about ten years younger than he really was, the oily skin within his face often hiding signs of impending change. All of this changed since Sam's death and he found that he could no longer thwart the signs of age, even though at only fifty five years old, he still had a good thirty or forty years ahead of him. It was his desire for life that was in question, owing back to the constant thoughts of whether he could really survive Sam's death, even after all of these years.

He began to question his own sincerity over the events of the past decade and the rationalization of his efforts to help people. *Was he really doing it for the benefit of mankind?* Perhaps something more sinister was behind his activities. Second guessing oneself frequently leads to questions, and his mind repeatedly sought out answers to puzzles that he had long since convinced himself of the solutions.

Sam was gone and he needed something to keep his mind occupied. She was a kind, loving individual and he just knew that he had to keep her memory alive by emulating her good deeds. Now he was entertaining thoughts of truly global change, read that intervention, and it was a track decidedly against anything that Samantha would've thought of. Help people, yes, but don't go too far beyond peaceful resistance towards cruel authority.

He had long since abandoned this last rule by launching direct, yet covert military operations against a host of small nations as well as a few large ones. Jason justified his actions as being a necessary evil, one that never, ever approached the cruelty of the leaders that he targeted. The good of the many, it was always said, was more important than the good of the one.

Now how to go about incorporating all of these conflicting goals? The thought raced through his mind, numbing his brain until the only solace found was plopping down deeply into his leather judge's chair and exhaling audibly. *Yes, how?*

The world didn't have a simple reset button which one could casually depress and begin a new civilization, ecosystem, and future. Neither did it require complete renovation; there was nothing inherently wrong with the world that he knew. The problem being the lack of effort on the part of the global leaders to enact realistic and effective management.

Countless nations, languages, cultures, and attitudes divided the planet. What was needed was unification, even if subliminal. Jason knew that a global government was, at best, a pipe dream. At worst, it spoke of world domination and slavery. Neither of which he wanted to launch upon an unsuspecting population.

For years, quietly at first, then slowly gaining credibility within his mind was the notion of a clandestine organization that could make adjustments to the status quo and give the world a nudge here and there. More secretive perhaps than Tactical Extractions, but not quite a cult as in many conspiracy theories. What was required, in his opinion, was a group of people who could sacrifice themselves in order to carry out the activities that the civilized world knew had to be done, but lacked the necessary balls to carry out.

Yes, this is what had to be done. He had to create a new organization that served no purpose but to protect the innocent, punish the wicked, and maintain the morality of a decaying planet.

2

THE NEW DAY arrived with intensity indicative of success and flooded the corner office with exquisite brilliance. Jason meandered through the room in a lazy, figure eight pattern oblivious to the visitor sitting silently in the far corner. His motions were on autopilot, but mental algorithms raced through his mind with the precision of a neurosurgeon, contemplating the implications of various actions and reactions.

"You know, Jack" he spoke after several more circuits of the floor. "I don't want to come across as some damn nut case, but I'm sick and tired of the way the world seems caught up within its own attitude. It's either sheep or wolves; no one in between. Not a damn person who sticks their head out and says 'Enough already, it's time for a change!' Not a damn person!"

"Well, the Pope and the President have been making statements." replied Jack Stephens, shifting his position in the oversized lounge chair. "The problem is that one is restricted by politics, the other by morality."

"Exactly!" Jason spun around on his feet, eager that his companion was thinking along the same lines as he. "The two most powerful people on the planet and they're hamstrung by position. Why can't there be someone who can step beyond the boundaries?"

"Shit, we've been doing a rather good job of that ourselves."

"I know, I know. But I'm talking about something a little different. It's one thing to race around the world and extract corporate executives from the clutches of whoever is trying to kill them, but it doesn't get to the root cause of the problem."

"Such as?"

"Such as eliminating the evil that forces people to accept such transgressions."

Jack rose slowly, stretching his sore muscles and proceeded to join his friend near the center of the room. "We *aren't* God; we can't eliminate evil from the world."

Jason paused in mid stride, lifting his left brow in reflection. "We can, however, punish those who *do* evil. We can lay the framework for an organization that just doesn't respond to evil after it's manifested itself within people, we can maintain a presence that guides people before they venture into its path."

"Aren't there a half million organizations that already attempt to do this?" laughed Jack as he parked himself on the corner of the desk. "The Mormons come to mind."

Jason ignored the humor and slowly walked over to the windows, not quite paying attention to anything that appeared outside. "I'm not a preacher. I don't want to be. What I want to do is improve the world so that we can evolve as a society, so that we can, should we find the balls to do so, venture out and discover other worlds, other planets, other civilizations. None of which can be accomplished if we sit around and think of ways of destroying ourselves."

"Profound, but is it practical?"

"Hell, I don't know." Jason turned to glance at his cousin, trying to determine his visitor's reactions to his thoughts. "It's going to happen some day, I suppose, otherwise we're going to be in a shit load of trouble."

"True."

"What I'm looking for is an organization that can respond in real-time to those threats that ordinary people come into contact with. Take those nuns, for example, wouldn't it have been better had *someone* stopped the kidnappings, tortures, and rapes *before* we had to move in and fry the place?"

Jack sunk his chin into his hand and nodded. "Yeah, but nobody can be in all places at all times."

A fresh thought illuminated the expression on Jason's face. "Maybe it's not necessary that we need to be in all places at all times? Maybe it would be sufficient that we are *thought* to be in all places at all times?"

"Meaning?"

"Listen, if you were a burglar and you struck at a particular neighborhood of, say, fifty houses. By random, you picked three to attack initially and all three fought back – the owners had guns or something. Anyway, wouldn't you be inclined to ignore the other forty-seven homes?"

"If I were still alive."

"Regardless, it would be the mere suspicion that the other homes were impenetrable. Now, if your criminal buddies heard that Jack the Nabber was nearly blown away while trying to rob the Joneses, Johnsons, and whomever else, wouldn't they be inclined to avoid this neighborhood?"

"Probably. I just don't quite understand what you're getting at. We can't teach six billion people to defend themselves, can we?"

"No. no." Jason retreated to his pacing the floor for a few minutes before pausing again. "Perhaps we just place people into key areas that can respond to events threatening those six billion people."

"We do that already, and it's costing us a fortune."

"No, we've been *responding*. We need to become more pre-emptive in our actions."

"Okay, someone looks like they're ready to do something bad and one of our guys blows them away. Will this be a *good* thing?"

"If we knew that they were ready to commit the crime, but this isn't exactly what I meant."

Jason returned to the windows, thinking of methods of conveying what his mind couldn't quite comprehend itself. His subconscious knew what he wanted; it just didn't share the information clearly with his conscious mind.

What he envisioned was an extension of his business, an organization that placed into existence barriers to problems before they materialized. An entity that was always *there* and known to the world even if they weren't allowed to know the who's, why's, and wherefores.

"Jack," he spoke with concern flowing down the crevices of his face. "The world is equally divided among good and bad, right and wrong, and practical and impractical. That much we know. There are many organizations that work against this problem. Take our beloved Catholic Church for example. It breathes holiness and concern for others. Still, there are people and organizations that are determined to destroy, or at least undermine, its efforts. These are the types of problems that our organization would overcome."

Now it was Jack's turn to pace the floor of the office. "We protect the protectors?"

"More like support. We have people all around the world and when, say, those nuns in Africa come under attack, we pounce on them. Sooner or later, people will simply start to suspect that we have more people than we really do."

"It sounds reasonable, but I suspect that you have more in mind than what you're letting on."

"I do. Unfortunately, it's more a feeling that I can't quite put into words. I know something is needed, but I just can't describe it or even rationalize about it. What do you think?"

Jack paused at the windows and casually observed a medevac helicopter dart across the horizon. "I think that the world is just going through a natural evolution of events that have been going on since time immortal, which leaves us just one of two choices. We can either sit back and let things work out for themselves, or we can undertake some action that could, at the very least, disrupt the natural flow of things."

"I agree." Jason returned to his desk, slowly sitting down into the plush chair as he retrieved a legal pad and pen to jot down some notes. He knew that he hadn't quite persuaded Jack as to his objective, but also knew that his cousin wasn't prone to leap into any plan that came along, even from him. "Let's consider the options more carefully."

"Sure." Jack retraced his steps back towards the corner. "First, if we do nothing-- the world goes on as it has. The First World War didn't stop the Second World War, which didn't stop Korea, which didn't stop the Cold War which unleashed terrorism which leads to Afghanistan, Iraq, Iran, Syria, North Korea..."

"And so on and so on..." interrupted Jason, trying to emphasize the point that Stephens was making on his behalf.

"Right. Simply put, the world generates its own wastes. Now, as to the second option. Suppose that we could, in fact, do something about it. This means we run the risk of creating a significant amount of trouble..."

"If things turn sour."

"Yes, if things go wrong. Let's assume that they go smoothly and we divert the direction of the planet. Then what? Are we prepared to assume responsibility for the future? Can we back away once the world learns to function on its own? Or, do we just become the latest in a long line of people who've fucked up this damn planet for years to come?"

Jason nodded quietly, but refused to comment.

"I think that I'm beginning to see where you're coming from." continued Jack. "You want to take a direct role in, shall I say, reining in this planet. You want to create some form of Utopia where medical supplies and food are delivered to those who need it. You want to have the ability and, for lack of better words, the *right* to remove anyone who stands in your way. In short, you want to play your version of God and damn everyone else. Your motives may be sound, but your methods are sour."

Jason grew a little angry over the lecture, but didn't show it. He knew that Jack was just playing the role of devil's advocate in order to flush out his cousin's subconscious thinking. They both knew each other too well to disbelieve anything they heard from the other.

"Okay, so what's your plan?" Jason stopped taking notes and concentrated on Jack's words.

"*My* plan? My plan is simply avoiding the complete destruction of the planet. We don't need that. No way. What I suggest is to civilize what we've already done with Tactical Extractions. We do everything on the sly, and I mean *everything*. We can't confront people directly. Sooner or later, they'll band together and eliminate *us* from the planet."

"All right. We remain secret. And?"

"Listen, our best hope for straightening out this damn planet is to persuade, not force. We train people who think, act, and believe in the same things that we do. We give them the technology and resources to remain within the local populations and, whenever anybody gets into trouble, they act and act swiftly."

"And what's so unusual about this? This is not much different than what we've been doing for years."

"Well, perhaps we now start protecting institutions as well as people. More specifically, we start protecting *selected* institutions. No more of this everyone has a say bullshit. We stick to those organizations and countries that align themselves with our way of doing things. First, and foremost, should be our protection of the Church which is being hammered from both the left and the right."

Jason cupped his hands behind his head and leaned back deeply into his chair. "We begin to actively promote a particular agenda?"

"Sure, we've done it already. Not to mention, we're both Catholics and we're both pissed as hell as to the way the rest of the world targets the Vatican, priests, the Holy Eucharist, you name it. If charity begins at home, then we begin with our core values. Period."

"We'd alienate a hell of a lot of people. I don't like it. Word gets out as to what we're doing and we've lost our support among the population."

"Well, we're not exactly liked now." Jack was well aware of Jason's hero image and this was the one thing that he didn't like about his friend. "Unsung heroes are the best. They do what they do because it is right, not because they want the glory. As for me, I believe in what I believe, and if we're really going to have an impact upon the world, we're going to have to stop playing games and make a stand. Otherwise, we're just two businessmen trying to manipulate the world for profit."

Jason chewed on his lower lip. What his cousin was discussing amounted to a crusade of sorts, an action that might be somewhat tolerated in the Americas or Europe, but if they encroached upon the Islamic world for example, complete mayhem might erupt. "We wouldn't be able to stop once we started."

"No, and that's why I'm not going to commit to this plan until we've had time to think things over and, consider the consequences to our families, friends, businesses, etc. What *are* our long term objectives and how much are we prepared to pay for them?"

"We've got a little soul searching to do." Jason knew that the implications were tremendous, but for the past thirteen years he had been on a collision course with destiny. Now he had to make a decision worthy of Napoleon himself. "Let's keep this quiet for now, and get back together next week."

"Agreed." Jack headed over towards the door, paused for a second, then turned back in Jason's direction. "Listen, if we do this, we don't pull any punches. We use maximum effort to unify the world's people. Screw Europe, screw the Islamist extremists. We don't permit revisionists to decide what's permissible or ethical. We make a stand as to what we believe and we evangelize like we're possessed. Then, we motivate this planet to migrate beyond our atmosphere so we can fuck up some other planet for a change."

JASON SPENT THE hour since Jack Stephens left in deep concentration, even ignoring his secretary who had showed up for work and brought him his newspaper and coffee before returning to the outer office to conduct her affairs. He had no idea if she offered any greetings and only became aware of her presence by the items that had mysteriously appeared on his desk.

Still, he remained in deep thought. Jack's final words reverberated in his mind like some medieval gauntlet thrown down by a crusader from centuries past. What his cousin presented was the end to the world as they had known it, perhaps even a greater modification than the collapse of the Soviet Union.

To simply indoctrinate the entire planet to a single set of beliefs was, well, extraordinary. It had been done before. The explorers settling the New World had done it and the radical Islamists of the current era were doing their best to accomplish this very same task.

What Jack proposed was to literally fight fire with fire. An all-consuming, all-purifying fire. It would end with either the destruction of the planet, at least their own little part of it, or it would be successful and unity would prevail. His money rested on the former.

Jason was more than a little unnerved by Jack's statement. It was uncharacteristic of the otherwise mild-mannered oceanographer whose research of the oceans captured worldwide attention and admiration. His darker side was kept pretty much secret as had Jason's. To openly talk about such things betrayed the presence of a deeper, more reflective individual.

Except for about ten years in age difference, both he and Jack could've passed for twins. Both stood about five foot eight, and kept their brown, balding heads shaved to within an eighth of an inch from nonexistence. Both had similar experiences and businesses, and both believed in the same values, politics, and opinions.

Therefore, it was mildly disturbing that Jack, the more subdued of the two, voiced what Jason had been holding within his mind for the past several weeks. To announce the idea, if not the actual practice, of re-inventing the world as it were, was something that rational businessmen simply did not do.

Sure, they modified the world extensively, all under the umbrella of Tactical Extractions' operations, but even that was strictly small scale. There was a world of difference between snatching captives away from a North Korean border town prison and orchestrating the downfall of entire nations.

The irony was that Jason hated crowds, and much rather spend his time up at his Wyoming ranch. An effort of this magnitude would place the world's six billion or so citizens squarely within his consciousness. He simply couldn't avoid shying away from their plight regardless of whether they figured prominently within any of his objectives.

Given this realization, he decided that it probably would be in his best interests if he were to head up to the Jagged T and remain secluded for a while. The thought that his actions, particularly ones such as this, might be something of a subconscious suicide wish played heavily on his mind.

Yes, he needed to head back up towards the ranch, spend time with the horses, deer, elk, bison, and the countless stars that shone down nearly every night. It would place everything into perspective and give him a chance to sort through the myriad of thoughts that raged through his mind. Most importantly, however, it would enable him to gain some much needed sleep.

3

THE JAGGED T occupied an L-shaped swath of prime grassland in the northeastern corner of Wyoming and provided home for several hundred head of bison, a corps of ranch employees, and solitude for one overworked executive.

Nearly eight square miles to a leg, the ranch was more than just an agricultural property, it represented salvation, peace, and a chance to kick one's feet up and unwind, and Jason always did just that.

Save for the sleepy towns of Gillette and Newcastle, as well as the expansive Thunder Basin National Grassland, there wasn't much of anything else in this part of God's Country, and that's precisely what drew Jason to this location.

He very much enjoyed being able to stare far out into the horizon, unobstructed by any artificial structures that in the name of art became anything but artistic in style. He felt peace whenever he found the need to venture into town as the locals treated him as a friend and neighbor instead of an employer or source of tax revenues.

At night, when the ocean of stars unveiled their majesty, he took comfort in knowing that there was a greater power behind all that lay before him. Frequently, he would ride one of his prized stallions out into the darkness and spy the Pleiades – the 'Seven Sisters', Number 45 in Messier's list of astronomical anomalies – shining overhead, or the constellation Ursa Major, the 'Great Bear' known to most of the world as the 'Big Dipper' directing his way towards the north. Each season presented its own list of friends and wonders.

Such journeys out into the pitch blackness of the Wyoming night offered a form of therapy to a man who still had trouble coming to grip with the loss of his wife. Out into the great expanse of the Jagged T, he could envision her presence and often talked to her, sharing his feelings, his thoughts, and his fears. He knew that she would never provide any answers, at least directly, but treasured the moments to unleash his concerns to his beloved confidant.

Far from being wealthy when they were together, he knew that she always loved the region and the ranch represented something of a tribute to her memory. More than any other asset, this ranch was protected by layers of legal protection; it would be the one asset that he would never dispose of, and he had good reason.

Isolated in the middle of the property was a clump of Cottonwoods nestled near a small pond, itself fed by a tiny stream. This small park-like setting represented the final disposition of Samantha's ashes, and the focus of his nocturnal journeys.

It was here that he felt closest to her presence, the physical spot where her spirit soared in his consciousness, and the only thing that he owned that he could comfortably believe that they *both* owned together. The existence of peace, solitude, and the 'physical' presence of his wife was something that he cherished immensely.

Even his trusted horses seemed to know that there was something very special about this spot, perhaps only by knowing that their master was a bit calmer here than in other areas of the ranch. Perhaps, however, they too could experience the presence of her soul, animals being somewhat closer to the reality of a Creator.

It was in times such as these that Jason needed, *really needed* the assistance of his wife. He had always valued her advice, even her scolding whenever he did something stupid. Now, however, when he literally had the burden of the entire planet resting upon his shoulders, he did not have the privilege of seeking her thoughts.

In a nation where half of the marriages land in divorce, Jason would've given his entire fortune for just a single day more with Samantha – twenty-four hours in which to thank her for all of those things that she did, that he never had time to, or somehow forgot to thank her for.

It was a burden that he imposed upon himself, for a small voice in his subconscious sometimes hinted at the possibility that Sam was up in Heaven, demanding that he get on with his life and find someone new. It was a thought that he aggressively tried to bury, but people are a social creature by nature, and no man was destined to be alone.

He knew this, knew it well. His salvation could only come from the presence of another soul mate, someone who'd share his passion for living, his respect for the unfortunate, and perhaps, just perhaps, give him the one thing that Samantha couldn't: children.

To create an empire to last a thousand years may certainly establish one's place in history, but a single offspring, particularly one that could carry on the family name, would be far more precious than any history altering enterprises and this was the one thought that he could not squash.

Time and time again, Jason reasoned, that the reason that God took Samantha away from him was that she could not provide him with any children. Therefore, he concluded, either he was meant to have children or that God, for some reason, had chosen to let him know that children weren't to be part of his legacy. He assumed the latter.

Success in business was small consolation for the loss of one's wife, to be sure, but he still accepted the challenge and considered it his life's duty to succeed. To create jobs, benefit communities, and promote his beliefs was his mission and he always undertook it with gusto.

If he were to *need* someone else in his life, then Sam would send someone to him, that much he was certain of. So, for thirteen plus years he built his business empire, stepping on a few people while he carried others, and ultimately succeeded in what he never thought possible during his dreamy days as a married man.

JASON DRAGGED HIMSELF out from underneath the quilt, hardly recognizing where he was for a few moments until the presence of the imported Canadian log walls in his master bedroom reminded him of his long night at the ranch. How long he had slept, he wasn't sure. The window panes blazed with a pearly white glow which only informed him that it was day. As to what time of day it was, he hadn't a clue and decided that the first course of action was a shower to remove the stench that emanated from his armpits.

His mind still clouded with jet lag and the results of an even longer journey from the airport, Jason staggered over towards the dresser to retrieve a fresh pair of briefs before heading into the bathroom. He ignored the drooping image that appeared in the mirror which towered over the dresser with a yawn and a careful scratch of his backside.

A nice, hot shower would be a blessing, he thought, and do much to erase the frustrations associated with the city. Walking into the bathroom he flung his shorts haphazardly onto the vanity and opened the glass door to the shower and started the water flowing.

Allowing the liquid time to heat up, he retrieved a can from the cabinet, squirt its contents into his right palm and slapped a sizeable clump of the shaving cream onto his cheeks, massaging the foam into a rich lather upon his face.

Next, he grabbed his razor from its holster next to the sink and stepped into the shower, allowing the warmth of the water to cascade down upon his sore shoulders, before beginning to mow the stubble that aged his face beyond his years.

He had to admit that he was close to cashing in the whole damn lot and remaining a simple cattle rancher for the remainder of his life, but he just couldn't keep his mind off of the discussion that he had with Jack Stephens.

There was something decidedly addictive about global intrigue and control, the ability to contemplate actions that would alter the course of history and the social welfare of billions of individuals. There had been a fire burning deep down in his consciousness regarding the implications of a complete overhaul of the world community. Something really drastic, something uniquely Jason Task in scope.

This plight was evident everywhere he looked, and it rested squarely upon the shoulders of procrastination. Americans landed on the moon in *1969* but by the twenty-first century they couldn't even get a manned vehicle off of the ground. President Nixon had declared war on cancer three decades earlier, but even today a person had little if any greater chance of surviving the disease. The examples were boundless.

Jason knew that most people had the attention span of a two-year-old and decisions weren't made until they were absolutely, positively required. So, he thought to himself, he would force the issue.

Completing his shave, Jason quickly rinsed off his face and washed his hair before turning off the water and grabbing the towel which hung casually on the shower door to dry himself. Perhaps, he continued to think, what was needed wasn't a destruction of the world, rather an analysis of what was *good* for the world. Left to their own devices, people only thought about what mattered to them and not anyone else.

The train of thought continued as he marched into the bedroom to pull on a pair of khaki slacks and a black knit shirt. The world needed to get its ass kicked. Not in the sense of another global conflagration, but perhaps a swift push in the right direction for motivation. Perhaps a leader, whether an individual such as him or an institution such as Tactical Extractions could serve as the catalyst.

People admired leaders, even tried to emulate them, but they never *obeyed* them, at least not completely. The President was bound by votes and the Pope by morals. Conscience is the archenemy of decision, which is why dictatorships were always efficient if not long-lived.

Jason's thoughts were beginning to clear as he worked his way down the long, twisting staircase into the large, open air 'Grand Room' which occupied the shell of the house, before heading into the breakfast nook which sat adjacent to the kitchen. The smell of a Denver omelet wafted throughout the room as he sat down at a small wooden table and soaked in the aroma.

"Something sure smells good." he spoke as his mouth watered, and his heart longed for a home cooked meal. "Real good."

"I thought that you'd want something special this morning." replied a shapely brunette from the kitchen, bringing out a full plate consisting of omelet, toast, grits, and orange juice.

"Juanita." replied Jason, smoothing the wrinkles out of the table cloth. "You're a doll. I don't know what I'd do without you."

The woman smiled, entertaining brief thoughts of marriage and companionship. "Just doing my job."

"Bullshit!" cracked her employer. "All of the money in the world would be insufficient to pay for what you do around here."

Juanita Wilson calmly sorted out her benefactor's breakfast, intentionally closing into his personal space so that she could smell the cologne that he frequently wore. "I do no different now than I did when you hired me five years ago."

"Has it been five years? Why, you look just a good as you did when I first saw you."

Juanita's skin flushed as she playfully smacked him with the dish towel that until then had been draped across her wrist. "Yeah, right. You know that I turned forty-five last week; you sent me the flowers." She kissed him on the top of his head. "Thanks."

"Well," replied Jason, somewhat embarrassed. "You can't get that good looking in less time."

"Thanks, Jace."

Jason paused in his eating, nearly shoving a fork full of omelet into his nose as he watched his cook's amply toned buttocks disappear into the kitchen. *Woah.* "Say, why don't you make one for yourself and join me?"

"I think I will."

After a few minutes, culminating with the same wonderful aroma that he first noticed, Jason observed Juanita return from the kitchen. The absence this time of her apron revealed more of her shapely figure tucked neatly into a white blouse and tight blue jeans.

"That's better." he spoke as she settled into her seat. "I haven't had a meal like this in a long, long time."

"You need to come around more." Juanita smiled, unfolding her napkin. "I'll keep you full."

Jason returned a wink. "Perhaps I better. You know that I don't get treated as well as I do here."

"Damn straight. You know very well that we take care of you up here. Not like those people down in Oklahoma City."

Jason played around slightly with his food. It was nice having a woman to kid around with, and it helped take his mind off of more disturbing things. In short, it made him feel more *human* than when he was down in Oklahoma running his business.

Juanita noticed his face turn more serious in composure, the tanned skin becoming more pale and tight. His few wrinkles becoming more prominent than they had only a few moments before. "Jace, why did you come up here yesterday?"

"Oh, I just needed a break." Jason hoped that she wouldn't ply any deeper, yet he also wanted her to talk with him. "You know, business."

"Uh, huh." Woman's intuition being what it was, Juanita knew that something was tugging at the mind of her boss. "It's terrible losing someone close, isn't it?"

Jason stopped playing around with his food and sat upwards in his chair, throwing his shoulders back in an act of recognition. "Yes, it is. How long has it been since your husband was killed?"

"Seven years."

"Oh, yes. I had forgotten."

"Well, life goes on, as they say."

"But how does one...how do *you* manage?"

"You just manage. Losing a spouse isn't easy for anyone, and you never, *ever* get over it. But you do go on."

"Perhaps." Jason redirected his gaze towards the side, avoiding direct contact with the sparkling blue sapphires that were her eyes. It was an awkward attempt to defend against a charming woman, a woman that definitely aroused his interests. "I don't think that I could.."

"Sure you could." Juanita didn't give him a chance to feel sorry for himself. "You just don't want to. At least, for now. But you will. Somewhere out there is someone that you'll fall in love with, maybe marry, and move on with your life. And you know something? She'll never take the place of your wife. She'll just be herself, earning your love on her own merits."

Jason nodded, allowing himself to glance back towards her eyes. "I don't know. It's been thirteen years. Maybe I'm just a basket case."

"It's been *only* thirteen years." Juanita reminded him. "Different people recover differently. Some remarry within six months. Some never do. Jason Task will do what Jason Task is supposed to do. You needn't worry about it."

"Perhaps you're right. I've just been so preoccupied with my damn businesses, organizations, you name it. Sometimes I feel like screaming 'Kiss my ass!' to the world. It's maddening, really."

Juanita moved over to Jason's side, knelt down and took his hand into hers. "Listen, Jace. I know you. I know you well. You're one of the most important people on this planet. You care about others. That's why you've created jobs, schools, hospitals... heck, the whole world owes you something. And you did it *after* you went through complete hell. You're frustrated because you want to do more, not because you've done any less."

Deciding to throw away any pretense of formalities, Jason pulled her up onto his lap. "Thank you. I could always count on you setting me straight. Perhaps, this is why I always feel comfortable up here."

"You're welcome." Standing up, Juanita started for the kitchen. "Why don't you go for a ride or something. Let loose for a change."

Jason thought long and hard about asking her to accompany him, but as she disappeared into the kitchen, he knew that she meant that he should go riding *alone*. He knew that he needed to work things out by himself, especially given the nature of the goals that he and Jack had set forth.

Savoring a quiet moment listening to his cook hum calmly in the kitchen, Jason rose and walked across the main room into his ranch office, selecting a seat next to a television and switched on the *Fox News Channel*.

The same, familiar stories ran. Someone was blown up in the Middle East, turmoil reined in the recently collapsed country of North Korea, and Europeans, as usual, blamed the United States for nearly everything. The troubles were predictable, only the players changed.

The world will destroy itself long before we get the chance to. The thought echoed in Jason's mind like a battle cry and he began to formulate a new plan, something between what Jack had talked about and what they were already doing through Tactical Extractions.

He spun around in the chair and shoved a stack of papers out of his way, turning off the television in the process. He didn't need any further distractions; he had a game plan to write down. Grabbing a nearby clipboard that held lined paper within its teeth, Jason began to scribble down his thoughts.

First, he knew, as great as Tactical Extractions was, it was still more or less a business operation. It wasn't a military organization anymore than it was a political party. What they needed was something that was both, but still clandestine in nature. Something that could influence without being influenced itself.

Tactical Extractions provided the technology and perhaps the manpower, but it wasn't set up to teach what had to be taught. It couldn't, by virtue of its nature, impact the thought processes of any individuals other than, perhaps, those that it directly affected.

Ultimately — and this was the first thought written down on the clipboard — they needed to control schools. Teach kids *your* way from grade school on and within twenty years, you have adults who think your way. Multiple this several thousand times and soon you have whole communities that think and act like you.

This idea wasn't exactly new or untried. The liberal teacher's unions had been carrying out this practice for decades. Now, Jason decided, it was time to use their methods against them.

The second thing that he wrote down concerned the Catholic Church. This fine institution, perhaps the world's very salvation, had been undermined from within by abusive priests, liberal theologies, and disinterested congregations. What was needed was an internal police force that cracked down on those who tried to re-interpret its laws. He knew that the Vatican wouldn't condone what he wanted to do, but he figured that they were going to do everything in secret anyway.

Next, he began to visualize something really big. He knew that they couldn't expect to make any radical changes to the planet. Yet, if they were to carry the idea of migration from this planet beyond the drawing board, if only in theory, then they could have a somewhat legal basis for picking and choosing people who thought along the same lines as they did.

Simply put, they could use business and technology as a means to screen out people that didn't quite match their expectations. While the rest of the world assumed that they had something extraterrestrial in mind, they would merely be using the ruse to reformulate Mother Earth. Techniques to train people to explore outer space could be used to train people to behave on the planet.

The same thing could be done with Jack's oceanographic company, perhaps more so. They could set up institutions to explore the deepest parts of the sea. The closeness of the inhabitants and the miles of water that separated them from dry land would prove invaluable in keeping outside influence at bay.

Slowly, ever so slowly, Jason began to picture the utopia that Jack had joked about. It wasn't an utopia in which everyone lived in bliss or perfection, but one in which their ideas mattered. Once people learned to get along with each other and valued the dignity of human life, *then* they could work on more astronomical objectives.

The planet, he was aware, was ripe for this kind of restructuring. There were people who believed in crop circles, alien visitations, and faked lunar landings. Why should it be any different with people who had at least some brains? Perhaps they could manipulate those who were, in his opinion, idiots, in order to ensure that rational, faithful individuals were the only ones that remained.

Somewhere he read, that there were only about two hundred people on the planet that actually controlled the rest of the six point whatever billion. He knew that he was one of the two hundred, so that left a hundred and ninety-nine. If he could exercise some level of control over these, then his plan would succeed.

Still, as every dictator, despot, and presidential hopeful knew, the masses were the ones who were the most dangerous. Revolutions always seemed to erupt from the streets, and Jason could not be successful without taking this simple fact of life into account.

Rolling his chair over to a computer, Jason logged on to the system and retrieved data regarding global agricultural sales, information that was used to gauge his cattle operations. Intently studying the colorful graphs and flashing codes, he saw what he was looking for. Weather forecasters were calling for heavy rains in both Asia and South America and the possibility for social unrest came to the forefront of his intuition.

Moving to the Internet, he quickly searched for those nations that were below the threshold of solvency – those nations whose agricultural production was far below that of their internal consumption. He then did a quick analysis of those neighbors whose production far exceeded their needs. Putting two and two together, he quickly thought of ways to instigate trouble between the neighboring countries. *Could this be an avenue for influence?*

Jason quickly turned his attention away from the computer. *No.* He would not instigate any wars or riots. They would have to find some way to participate in troubles already begun. In fact, he decided, they would become the *saviors* of the trouble spots, not their proponents. Only then could they gain influence among the local populations.

"Feed sheep." Jason mumbled quietly. "And they will follow you everywhere."

4

JASON GUIDED THE immaculate palomino along the well-worn path that snaked like a rattler through the midsection of the ranch as it snorted impatiently at the herd of bison grazing off in the distance. The steady wind that charged unceasingly against his face burnishing his exposed skin blew whirlwinds through the flowing Bermuda grass creating the impression of sea waves.

He adjusted the smoke gray cowboy hat that seemed as uncharacteristic on him as a fedora would in its place. So, for matters of protocol, he wore the appropriate article of clothing for the current situation, regardless of how uncomfortable it made him feel.

For those infrequent periods when he was caught outside in a downpour, the stylish headpiece did in fact serve its purpose and drain the water away from him, so he became accustomed to its presence whenever he visited Wyoming. Like a good pair of boots, when a hat fits, it *fits*.

His mind was heavy with thoughts, and the ride through the grasslands was the only way that he could clear his head and work out the problems that nagged unceasingly at his sanity. The primary burden being that he could never allow himself to become apathetic once a problem presented itself. It just wasn't how he became successful in business.

The world was a powder keg of instability and problems, everyone knew that, but the solution to these problems was an oft debated pretext for international negotiations. Something, however, had to be *done* and done quickly. Jason didn't want social evolution to become simply a spectator sport.

He had more or less decided on the schooling option, primarily for those citizens based in developing nations where most of the social strife was concentrated. By giving those children a decent, respectable education founded on solid moral principles, they would spread out through their respective countries as the children aged into adulthood. It was a long-term prospect, sure, but he had to head off the ravages of modern culture early, before they took hold.

It was a fundamental discrepancy between terminologies; most people believed that God had given them freedom instead of *free will*. The former absolved one from any form of responsibility; the latter required the acceptance of responsibility for one's actions.

In America, for example, the common view that one could do whatever one wanted to do without consequences made such actions almost expected. Jason knew, as did his friend and cousin Jack, that people had to weigh the implications of their actions and judge themselves accordingly. Yes, God permitted people to do whatever *they* decided to do, but the final conclusion could be nothing less than a choice between Heaven and Hell.

As he nosed his stallion over to the creek for a quick drink, Jason knew that this eternal battle between freedom and free will also applied to him. Yes, he could virtually annihilate the planet with his resources. Yet, was *he* prepared to accept final judgment?

He reflected upon the old television cartoons of a devil and an angel sitting on some poor character's shoulders, instigating him into one course of action or another. *How apropos.* His thought turned towards the implications of not doing anything. Perhaps God would hold him accountable if he didn't use his resources to inflict such a change upon the world. Why was he given such wealth now?

The horse completed his drink, and without prodding from its owner, elected to move further along the trail to the other side of the pond. This was normal, as Jason was often carried along by the animal as much as the animal was guided by its rider. While on the trail, they were one, and wherever one decided to go, they other went along willingly. If only people behaved as such, Jason amused to himself.

A flock of Canadian geese broke the air with their shrill call, launching off towards the southeast, but he didn't bother noticing. The ranch was both deafening quiet and breathtakingly loud, but what it wasn't was artificial. The loudest roar of a stampede would've been more peaceful than the constant din of the city.

Jason rode near a solitary bull standing a distance from the main herd and reflected upon the omen. A single individual standing out from the crowd but with their full future within his power. The bison obviously ignored his surroundings; he knew that he was king of the land.

Nature always gave examples to humans, but the so-called intelligent species rarely bothered to read the messages. Simplicity was considered abnormal and by the time people got it right, much devastation laid behind.

A theory that Jason held was that things really started to go down hill, in America at least, with the legalization of abortions. Ever since then, he figured, a culture dedicated to the destruction and *de-humanization* of life began to develop. Everything from pornographic television shows to women being allowed to serve in combat to embryonic stem cell research could be traced to that singular event, the pivotal case in whether America continued to be a great nation or just another in the long line of civilizations that, like the mythical Atlantis, rose to greatness only to be destroyed by greed, lust, and internal conflict.

More than anything else, Jason realized years ago, abortions needed to be stopped. Yet, open conflict went directly against the preservation of human lives that he bound himself to. His covert military actions were conducted under a single premise: protect *innocent* human lives at all costs. This meant that his teams did not target any individual who wasn't in the direct process of harming, or preparing to harm, innocent parties.

The case had been made that, according to this rule, abortion doctors were in the process of killing innocent babies, but Jason vetoed the measures under the presumption that, as heinous as these procedures were, they were still *permitted* under the present laws of the United States.

So, armed with this simple but disturbing fact, Jason relied heavily upon legal methods for fighting the abortionists who tried to sneak into the legal system under the secular term *Pro-Choice* as if it were some decision any reasonable person could make. By funding television commercials, daycare centers, infant hospitals, etc., Jason did everything within his power to defeat this most pronounced of social injustices.

Still, the world drifted away from the sanctity of life and, before long, South America began to slide into the same secular, post-Christianity system of beliefs that sent once proud Europe spiraling into decay. Only Asia, it seemed, stayed loyal to the traditions of family responsibility and Jason wondered how long that would last.

Given this realization, he decided that legal methods were no longer feasible, in particular since the activism apparent within U.S. courts seemed to, at best, delay *good* decisions until it was too late for them to be effective.

It was at this moment that a historical tidbit from the 1800's figured prominently in his thoughts. The exploits of the abolitionist John Brown were morally wrong and illegal, but the results weren't. The nation was forced to confront the issue of slavery and what it took to end that disgrace.

Jason knew that another civil war was out of the question, but the nation was still as equally divided along the lines of Pro-Life and Pro-Abortion as it was with Abolitionism and Slavery. Though he could not fight within the United States proper, he could carry the fight on by proxy elsewhere, using the same methods that the Soviet Union and the United States used during the Cold War. To avoid the destruction of their own countries, they chose to fight each other on foreign soil.

He would have to follow along a similar tack. By targeting nations for which he owed no allegiance, he could isolate the policies of the one country that he was trying to change. Only the United Nations would stand in his way and he was so disgusted with this sorry assed organization that, privately, he hoped for a showdown of some sort.

In view of all of this, he was beginning to forge out his confidence in both his ambition and his methods. He would protect innocent human life throughout the world with all of his abilities and resources and pay no concern to the existing administrations of those countries that he had to target. It was a decision that bordered on sacrilege, but someone had to undertake what God seemed reluctant to do.

Whereas Tactical Extractions catered to isolated individuals with the resources to pay a hefty premium for their rescue, his new organization would apply this service to those who probably could not even afford a decent meal. In short, he would extend his services to the entire population of the planet.

This would be a major undertaking, the most massive project that he ever attempted. Undoubtedly, he'd never live to see the fruits that his efforts sowed, but this was no different than being a parent. For the moment, he thought, this was his legacy, his child, his offspring. Whatever history remembered of Jason Task, it would be because of this new role in its future.

He glanced at the Rolex strapped to the underside of his left wrist. It was 2:33 P.M. He glanced around the ranch, instinctively knowing that he would not spend as much time here for awhile, and felt a urge of homesickness. He desired to stay, to spend time with his horses, to frequent the tiny park where Samantha's remains were scattered, and, quite by chance, developed a slight urge to spend more time with Juanita.

Jason's appointment with destiny, however, would intervene in the most cruelest way. He had chosen to make an impact on the world, a significant impact. One that would alter the course of history as no other event could. First, however, he needed to call in the troops.

5

JACK STEPHENS SAT in his Palm Bay, Florida study going through an unstable stack of books, several of which slipped off of the top and crashed down onto the parquet floor. He hadn't time to bother with them and eagerly sought out the one text that mattered most at the moment.

It had been an hour since he received an urgent email from Jason with the news for a major undertaking, and he needed the notes that he had tucked inside of the volume, hand scribbled locations of various equipment depots that may come in handy.

After a frantic ten minute search, he found the slip of yellowing paper buried deep within a text on the locations of sunken nuclear subs. He had been toying with the idea of attempting to retrieve plutonium from the stricken vessel's weapons systems, but decided that the venture was too risky and expensive.

Now, based on the information from his friend, that project sounded a hell of a lot less expensive and difficult than what they were planning to accomplish. Jason wanted to establish schools, a lot of schools, at various locations throughout the developing world. He also wanted to take a hand in the economic infrastructure of these nations, all with the intent of selectively guiding their development into what he called, "Our way of doing things."

The school idea sounded plausible and would go a long way towards their ultimate goal, but it would still take decades before the first results were achieved. To change the course of history, however, required something more near-term and powerful. Jack had replied back that he would work on the school project as a secondary mission, but that he'd come up with something a little more drastic, a little more pronounced in an effort to jumpstart their policies.

Almost from the moment they first spoke in Oklahoma City, Jack had developed an idea that was, at once, military, political, economic, and social in nature – all the key ingredients that were required by 'The Mission' as they now referred to it. To launch this initial idea required a host of military and industrial hardware, the very items that existed on the nearly lost slip of paper.

For years, Jack had his eyes on the newly created nation of South Sudan, the former southern provinces of the Republic of Sudan whose inhabitants were overwhelmingly Christian. After years of neglect by the impotent United Nations and other European organizations, this newly formed republic finally had an opportunity to break away from the Islamic northern regions of Africa.

What South Sudan lacked, unfortunately, was a military, a police force, an economic base, and recognition from a vast majority of the other nations of the world. What they had, however, was *hope* and a mysterious benefactor in the United States by the name of Jack Stephens.

Once Jason had brought up his ideas in Oklahoma, Jack immediately thought about stepping up his efforts in Africa and making a more public, more substantial effort to turn that tiny nation into something that could be used as a base of operations.

For their purposes, South Sudan was ideally located. It occupied an area that served as a border between the Christian nations to the south and the Islamic belt to the north. Airfields constructed in this country could support activities ranging from the Algerian-Libyan border on over to the Persian Gulf – a huge chunk of Muslim real estate.

Democratic developments within this region could be supported with troops, supplies, medicines, and nearly everything else that could sway popular opinion in their favor, save for the decidedly problematic thought of having help provided by a *Christian* nation. There were, fortunately, ways around that obstacle.

Aside from the strategic location of South Sudan, and the ease at which supplies could be forwarded into the country from the south,

Jack's petroleum operations were already established in most of the target nations, providing the intelligence infrastructure that they required to move into these countries at some point in the future.

Less enigmatic perhaps, were the vast mineral rich nations to the south that were politically dicey to begin with and weren't in direct conflict with the Islamic neighbors to the north. A move into these areas would shore up their financial resources while stabilizing a significant portion of one of the world's foremost trouble spots.

By controlling a swath of African real estate from the White Nile in the north to the Kalahari Desert in the south, they would have access to a territory equaling the continental United States in area. Such a bold venture may have seemed improbable, but as Jack always mentioned, hardly anybody was concerned about what went on in Africa.

This sad state of international relations would work to their benefit. McIntyre Pharmaceuticals had been pumping new medicines into the region to assist with the fight against AIDS, Ebola, and a broad spectrum of other deadly diseases. Most Africans already knew that Jack was on the people's side.

Similarly, an European affiliate of the Offshore Division of Stephens Oceanographic had been assisting with the development of a massive new desalination plant near Mogadishu, Somalia. An expansion of the plant combined with the installment of a water pipeline into the heart of central Africa would provide the local populations with an abundance of clear, fresh, healthy drinking water.

Jack kicked his feet up onto his desk, nearly knocking over what was left of the stack of books and took a long, cool sip from the Diet Coke® that sat heretofore idle on a coaster near the corner of his computer credenza. The thoughts that flew through his mind were intoxicating to say the least, and he enjoyed every minute of the rush.

Since a child, he had mentally devoured everything military, and was fond of reading about the histories of Alexander the Great, Attila the Hun, and nearly every campaign up to the present. Having only served within the Navy as an Electrician's Mate during the heightened Cold War years of the 1980's did little to dissuade him from taking a more active role in military conflicts later on.

This was not to say that Jack Stephens was merely an armchair general or a war monger. In reality, he was a calculating risk taker with a stringent conscience that would only undertake a mission if it had some form of benefit. This was difficult, for he knew that societal evolution by way of armed conflict was something of a dying habit. Civilization could only mature through inspired evolution and in this case, it meant progress through migration. Waging war was therefore no longer advisable for influencing people; its sole function was to *remove* barriers or other obstacles that stood in the way of progress much in the same manner as an old structure was demolished before a new building could take its place. By accepting war as a necessary means of punishing those individuals or institutions that indiscriminately harmed innocents, Jack found that his morals did not stand in the way and he fought his battles with conscience. That is, to say, that he fought without regard to the constant bickering and second guessing that plagued Western armies, much in the same way that General Tecumseh Sherman fought his battle through the South while still acknowledging that "War is Hell!"

While mentally going through the various scenarios regarding South Sudan, Jack spied one of the texts that had laid on the floor, a casualty of the collapse of books that marked his search for the supply list. It was a reprint of a hardly published volume regarding a mysterious band of crusaders known simply as the Gatestrian Knights.

He leaned forward and retrieved the book, tapping it against his palm lightly in recognition of the story behind these brave and chivalrous souls. If memory served him correctly, these knights did not just partake in the Crusades to destroy and pillage; they accepted the culture, if not the faith of the Arabs and tried to infuse Christian dogma with cultural exploration.

What earned their respect from Jack was that they didn't forfeit their Christian beliefs in the name of conquest. They didn't turn into ravaging animals in order to accomplish their mission. Instead, they upheld their respect for women, innocent lives, and reverence for God. Jack smiled as he very carefully thumbed through the pages of the obscure text before placing the book back onto its shelf, selecting a prominent place for display. They would do well to practice the beliefs of the Knights. Any objective, whether insignificant or epic, has at its base both a method and a result. To know how one gets to where their going is as important as the destination itself. Jack knew that it would be insufficient merely to plan for the salvation of human souls or the stability of the planet. Once that much had been achieved, civilization itself would undoubtedly decline due to stagnation.

He was equally aware of the Ming emperors of fifteenth century China whose reluctance to permit their admirals to round the Cape of Good Hope — thereby eventually discovering Europe — ultimately permitted Europeans to discover China and emerge as the dominant civilization for centuries to come. The decision to halt such explorations on the basis that nothing worthwhile would be discovered sent Chinese culture into a death roll from which it still hadn't recovered.

Like Jason Task, Jack always thought *big* and considered implications well into the future. If they had to go through the hassle of unifying the planet along moral lines, then they couldn't allow it to fall back into the same trap as did the Chinese in centuries past. The world had to be given a mission that would not dissipate in a matter of time. Simply put, the world needed to evolve *ad infinitum*.

For this to happen there could be only one of two solutions. Either it had to expand into the seas or into outer space. Perhaps both. Jack's business steadfastly promoted the former, but he was also intelligent enough to realize that as massive as the oceans were, they were still finite in size and sooner or later would lose their appeal. No, for a world to develop along truly astronomical proportions, it had to look *up*.

This realization in itself posed significant hurdles. For the cost of a single satellite launch, he could build a huge cruise ship that could house thousands of people and employ hundreds more. To change this meant to mass produce technologies to lower cost, fly them routinely so as to progress rapidly, and find some way of getting *hundreds* of people into space quickly.

This, undoubtedly, would be a task for generations to come. His purpose, for the present, was to create a society that could contemplate such adventures beyond the realm of science fiction. A civilization that could undertake such macro-engineering projects as the pyramids, the cathedrals of Europe, and the Panama Canal. Difficult, yes, but not impossible.

What the world required was a motivational leader, once whose respect and admiration had been earned and not forced upon the population. Someone who could make bold claims that the world would believe solely because he had the tact, intelligence, and brass balls ego to carry them out. Jack's mind floated back towards the days of the early Howard Hughes. He was just such a man, and Jack also knew of another such individual.

6

"DO YOU HAVE the necessary equipment on site?" Jason's voice was muffled and could barely be heard above the roar of the brilliant blue and sea green Sikorsky S-92 helicopter which had just landed aboard the crude tanker *Task Enterprise II*.

Jack nodded, giving his best effort to keep his hat from flying overboard. "Yes, we've got C-130's flying the teams in now." Once he escorted his friend away from the danger zone, he reached over and shook Jason's hands. "I've also got supplies coming in across the border from Kenya."

"Good." Jason moved quickly towards the towering superstructure, away from the disturbance of the helicopter as it lifted back off to begin the hundred mile journey back towards Cape Canaveral in the west. "We need to make sure that we double our efforts, even triple them so that South Sudan doesn't fail."

Jack led his companion towards the vessel's island, up several decks until they came to a door that led inside to the opulent owner's stateroom, waiting for Jason to enter before sealing the hatch behind them.

"I took the liberty of sending in more advisors along with the teams." Jack motioned towards a table on which sat a series of colorful topographic maps, globes, and satellite images. "I want this operation to be significantly more advanced than what I had been conducting in the past."

Jason nodded a cursory acknowledgement; he had already been fully briefed on board the helicopter via telephone link. He quickly moved over to the table and retrieved the latest satellite images, knowing instinctively which ones to analyze. "It looks like the Sudanese to the north don't suspect anything different. They've got the same troops stationed at the same locations."

"Not yet." cautioned Jack. "Sooner or later though, someone's gonna notice a shit load of C-130J's flying in regularly and know damn well it's not humanitarian supplies."

"No, no they wouldn't. Still, we can get some reinforcements in before they get wise. What about artillery?"

Jack reached over for a small red binder to jog his memory, and flipped through the pages until his found what he searched for. "We're sending 155mm howitzers over the border in shipments labeled agricultural and industrial equipment, mostly at night when the guards are tired and preoccupied with getting to sleep."

"Good. I don't want to start anything unless we're attacked. Remember, this is supposed to be a covert buildup. Any wind of this and everything's going to erupt into a full-scale war and our asses will be hung out and fried."

"Don't worry." reassured Jack. "I'm not interested in starting a Holy War against our friends in the north. I just want to ensure that South Sudan will remain a viable base of operations for our purposes."

Jason studied the maps intently. South Sudan was a tiny nation whose northern border was the White Nile, while Ethiopia, Kenya, Uganda, the Democratic Republic of Congo — which rotated its name with Zaire frequently, and the Central African Republic combined to form its remaining borders. In short, the tiny new nation was surrounded by larger and more powerful neighbors who'd take exception to any outside interference.

"Yeah, I know what you're thinking." replied Jack rather intuitively. "Tiny ass country right smack in the middle of the world's bitch spot and our finger prints will be all over it."

"Yeah."

"Well, once we move in our teams, they won't be so defenseless. Protection breeds security, security breeds economic potential, economic potential breeds strength."

Jason had come equipped with his game face and didn't show a hint of nervousness regarding the speed at which things were beginning to unfold. He had long since forgotten about the Jagged T, Oklahoma City, or even his enjoyable breakfast with Juanita. He was now in charge of a major operation which could lead to a premature eruption of hostilities and such thoughts had no business being at the forefront of his consciousness.

"It will be getting dark there soon." Jack spoke as he glanced at the clock that hung on the far bulkhead. It was 11:02 A.M. — 6:02 P.M. in South Sudan. "We'll be stepping up our penetration missions in a couple of hours."

"Right. Phase One should be completed by daybreak. Hopefully, the Sudanese won't notice much, but let's have everything stand by on Condition Red just in case."

Both men knew that they were now moving beyond the simple planning stages and any paramilitary buildup in South Sudan would not only place the new republic in a hazardous situation but wouldn't be tolerated by its larger, more powerful neighbor to the north, and the last thing that they needed right now was open conflict with an established, if not civilized, nation.

To help build a nation was one thing, to covertly manipulate an entire region was something else altogether. Jason knew that a major base in South Sudan was of paramount importance to their activities within the entire African-Middle Eastern theater of operations and any detection of their presence would initiate retaliation from at least one bordering nation and force their hand to move in deeper.

Given this reality, they had to move everything under false pretense. Of course, the newly elected South Sudanese government had no real objections to the presence of Jack's forces – no nation openly turns down military assistance – but once everyone else became aware of the situation they'd drop their backing of his forces like a bad habit. Therefore, there was a sense of urgency to provide enough manpower and equipment to significantly increase that nation's military strength prior to anyone else taking notice.

Jack picked up a pen and walked alongside the table tapping the instrument against its top in a rhythmic fashion. "You plan for these things time and time again, but whenever they come, you second guess yourself to the hilt."

Jason smiled, knowing that he was working with one of the best in the business, and walked over to pat his friend on the shoulder. "Just wait 'til we really start going. This is still small scale."

"Don't remind me." Inadvertently snapping the pen in two within his hand, Jack looked over at Jason with the look of one who had just received a bad omen, but said nothing further.

Jason shrugged his shoulders. *Better to break a pen than destroy our operation.* "We'll be making history."

Jack could care less about history; he wanted to improve the world. Moving military forces, especially *private* military forces, into a hostile region was just asking for trouble. Never mind that they had the covert blessings of the South Sudanese government and good relations with just about everyone to the south and east.

Africa was one of those strange places where everyone had an interest but nobody wanted to admit it. Only Egypt to the north had a long, interesting history that included everyone from the pharaohs to Emperor Napoleon to modern day tourists. As far as the rest of the continent was concerned, however, interest began to fade with the collapse of apartheid in South Africa.

An entire land mass ripe with disease, ethnic cleansing, and with its past eternally wrapped within the stench of slavery had no expectations but to be abandoned by the rest of the world. As with other hard luck cases, it occasionally drew the attention of do-gooders such as rock stars and super models, but for the most part what happened in Africa remained off the front pages, and this is just what Jason Task hoped would continue to be the case.

The Republic of South Sudan was to be an experiment, a proving ground beyond the laws of civilized gentlemen where their techniques and equipment could be tested and evaluated prior to application elsewhere in the world. It was selected because it had the right mix of strategic location, available resources, and relative isolation. It also afforded a limited, but still useable, element of humanitarianism which might come in handy should the need arise for diverting a hostile world opinion.

Regardless, South Sudan was Jack's baby. Jason wanted to develop more social programs such as his schools, along with hospitals, factories, farms, and anything else that could win the hearts and minds of the continent. Having done that, *then* he would be receptive to open military actions against potential belligerents.

It was Jack's assurances that nothing beyond what was already being done would be attempted that persuaded his friend to include the tiny country within their game plan, but only as a base of operations and not as a major combat zone.

What made Jason feel a little uncomfortable with the current situation was that unlike his efforts with Tactical Extractions, they intended to remain in South Sudan for an extended period. This was a significant step beyond the 'jump in and grab 'em' procedures that were employed before, and the feelings that he felt were much like whenever he opened a new business and could not spare his attention elsewhere.

"Will we still be in business five years from now?" he quipped, almost to himself.

"What?" questioned Jack. He didn't quite hear what was said as he had been preoccupied with going over notes which were scribbled haphazardly on scattered stacks of index cards.

"Oh, nothing. Just thinking to myself, I guess."

"Relax, partner. I've got ten C-130J's on standby to pull our men out in case this thing goes off the deep end."

"What about all of our equipment?"

"Oh, I've got some plans for their destruction should it come to that." The smirk on Jack's face told Jason that his friend did in fact have a plan prepared to *sanitize* the place should events go against them.

"Yeah, I know you and your love of explosives. You're a weird son of a bitch!"

"You're the one that started Tactical Extractions and, if I recall, you've had to bail out of many areas before and they weren't exactly smoking because of camp fires when you left either."

Jason was in a corner. He did know the routine – always have an out whenever things didn't go well and this was no different. He amused himself with the thought of what possible effort Jack would have to make to eliminate any trace of their involvement in South Sudan.

All things considered, Jason was still an organizer, a person who liked to put programs into motion and then move on to the next project. Between the two, Jack Stephens was the one who always enjoyed the dirty work, a natural facet of his oceanographic experiences. At times, such as now, it nagged at Jason as if he wasn't pulling his weight, or more appropriately, that he was constantly fighting a battle between letting his emotions take over and keeping his conscience intact.

He always feared what would really happen if he lost the battle and returned to his pre-Samantha way of thinking – no holds barred against the world. She civilized him, tamed him. Made him what he was to become, even though fate intervened to make sure that she wasn't fortunate enough to have witnessed his meteoric rise to fame and fortune.

Jack noticed his friend's lack of focus, the sense that his mind disappeared somewhere in the wake of the massive vessel. "Let's step out for some fresh air. Shall we?"

The two men walked out through the hatch into the bright Atlantic sunshine and rested their arms against the yellow railing, neither speaking for several long minutes as each delved deeply into his own conscience. Jason, stared off into the distance as if he was searching for his ranch while his cousin spat defiantly into the ocean waves far below.

"You know, Jack." Jason finally spoke, still oblivious to the fact that they were a hundred plus miles off shore. "If the opportunity ever rose where we could bail out of this without getting in trouble, I'd be pretty damn tempted to take it."

Stephens nodded with polite resignation. "And I wouldn't blame you."

"You wouldn't?"

"No."

"Why?"

"I know you too well. You've been at this game for almost ten years now, thirteen since you paid the highest price anyone could and still be around to argue the matter. That's got to be hard. I sure as hell wouldn't know what to do if something happened to Jamie. As far as I know, you haven't made any errors in judgment to date."

"I wonder."

"Stop torturing yourself. You've made billions in less time than most people take to finish college and you never attended! That's got to amount to something! So you second guess yourself sometimes. Who the hell cares? You're just being thorough, and half of this damn planet owes you something anyway. So don't worry too much about moral issues. Do what's in your mind and in your heart and you'll never be punished for it."

"Oh, really?" Jason knew that he was his own worst critic and would never take matters lightly, especially when human lives were at stake.

"Really." Jack spat again into the ocean as if to show Mother Nature his stance on the issue. "We're in charge, and we're gonna make the rules now."

Jason curled his lips in on each other but stopped short of chewing them off. "What the hell, so we fuck up the planet. Who's going to notice?"

Stephens smiled, yanked open the hatch leading inside and motioned for his friend to enter. "We should be receiving the satellite link now from the frontlines."

The two businessmen-turned-tacticians entered the massive vessel and headed over to the ship's Communications Room which had been enlarged to house additional equipment uncharacteristic of a commercial vessel at sea. Few visitors to the *Task Enterprise II* bothered to notice the array of Silicon Graphics workstations that filled the center of the room, apparently assuming that they were standard equipment. They were anything but.

The *TEII* was Tactical Extraction's offshore office and command center, and it even had the luxury of having its own satellite system, *Extractstar*, which provided a secured link for communicating directly with personnel in the field. The primary satellite being so large – Jason's aerospace company operated the only true Heavy Lift Launch Vehicle in world inventory – that ground personnel could communicate worldwide with a device smaller than a standard cellular telephone.

7

TY MONROE SLID across his belly into the shallow trench that hid the presence of his team, timing his breathing with his movement so that he would be able to listen to his surroundings whenever he stopped.

After several minutes of concentrated effort, he was able to duck behind the large clump of dirt that permitted the men to sit upright without fear of detection from the north.

"A brother's got to be fuckin' mad to be sitting here quietly." Ty spoke, failing to keep his voice below a mere whisper. "Why'd we gots to be stayin' put anyways?"

"Because the man says so." replied a distinguished looking black man, his face wholly hidden behind a night vision scope. "They say 'Stay.', we stay."

"Ain't right." grumbled Ty, removing a pebble that had been lodged within the shaft of his left boot. "We'd never stayed put before."

"This isn't before." Jeff Brown momentarily lowered his night scope, carefully massaging the dryness out of his eyes. "We're told to stay and there's a reason we're staying."

Ty took a swig from his canteen, then swung his M-16A4 rifle over the edge of the trench, facing it towards the north. "Just don't feel right. Not at all."

Jeff ignored the younger, more inexperienced soldier and took another look through the scope towards the north. It was quiet, eerily quiet. A half an hour had passed since they observed a Sudanese patrol stop not a hundred yards from their position and then move on into the night.

The absence of the Sudanese didn't worry him as much as did the absence of his own patrol that had moved out an hour earlier. He had tried briefly to reach them via the radio, and then the satellite phone, but to no avail. Now, he was concerned whether he, Ty Monroe, Bill Graves, and John Mullen should pull out of the trench and head back across the border into South Sudan.

The fact that there were no gunshots was a fairly good sign, but he remembered the incident four years ago when two of his team were silently eliminated with knives and it took weeks to ascertain their whereabouts. He never wanted to repeat the trauma of telling a pregnant wife that her husband was lying mutilated in some despicable hellhole again.

A broad shouldered man with wiry red hair crawled over to his team leader and positioned his mouth near to his ear to avoid making undue noise. "Want me to see if I can find Jennings' outfit."

"No!" replied Jeff Brown authoritatively. "Nobody moves. Period."

"I just don't like it!" squirmed Ty, moving closer to the protective hill. "I got this feeling."

"Nobody moves, nobody says a goddamn thing." Jeff slid over towards the right side of the small dirt hill, more to move away from the incessant nagging of his rookie than as a means of gaining greater visual advantage of his surroundings. He knew that his rookie was scared — they all were — but none of them had to learn their assignment by remaining within a field of action for nearly two weeks without moving as had he.

Still, Ty had proved useful before, even exceptional, but those were dash and snatch operations where youthful energy could prove advantageous, not detrimental. This mission was different, and they were under orders from the top to say put and not let *anything* get south of them without their knowing about it.

The disappearance of Chet Jennings' four-man team and the unknown whereabouts of the Sudanese patrol made them all a little nauseous, and just a little bit irritated. They had been trained as a quick response recon team and now they were sitting idle in the field playing a game of wait and see with virtually no one else around.

Team Leader Brown dragged over an olive drab and dark brown nylon backpack that had laid underneath a pile of field rations and unzipped its large side pocket, displaying a hardened laptop computer and quickly set about entering commands for a satellite image of the location. With the speed and dexterity of a seasoned stenographer, he uploaded the algorithms that would command the rapidly approaching *SkyAction* satellite to conduct a multi-spectral wide field scan of the immediate area.

He hoped that such images would either help him pinpoint the location of his missing team, or clarify the locations of suspected hostiles in order to permit an evaluation of search and recovery options.

The projected path of the spacecraft showed as a black line against a red background to protect his visual acuteness at night, and he selected images of 1 meter resolution beginning from ten kilometers towards the north. To calibrate the sensors, he instructed the spacecraft as to their precise position via the Global Positioning Satellite System so that it could lock on them, and search for other targets that matched their spectral signature.

Jeff finished entering the commands, and then quickly checked the time. Twenty minutes. Twenty minutes before the high flying satellite would soar overhead and hopefully provide some answers to his multitude of questions. Silently, he longed for a reconnaissance aircraft, even a tiny one, so that they could have nearly instantaneous coverage of the area but that was a luxury that he forfeited when he left the Marines.

Prior to leaning back against the hill and impatiently waiting for the images to be beamed down to him, he sent a direct message to the folks waiting on the *Task Enterprise II*, bypassing several layers of his chain of command. It simply read: DEVELOP AERIAL RECON CAPABILITY, PLEASE.

ONE HUNDRED AND ninety-three kilometers above the African plains, the *SkyAction* satellite zoomed towards its target. Its path carried it over Minsk, Belarus, near Kiev, Ukraine, over the Aegean and Mediterranean Seas, and finally entered the continent over Egypt.

Near the town of Kaka, Sudan, it began beaming pulses of electromagnetic energy through the clouds until they struck their target and bounced back up towards the spacecraft's antenna to be transferred into digital code for transmission back down to waiting ground stations.

Similarly, its spinning mercury-based primary mirror sought out precious emissions of infrared and visible light, digitized this information, and strapped the data to the carrier bandwidth for the ride back down to earth.

As with any other machine, the satellite merely did what it was instructed to do, but with a hint of originality, the *SkyAction* Artificial Intelligence program snuffed out that data which it determined as being corrupt or otherwise unusable, sending only quality images to the teams in the field. The damaged data instead was flashed to a ground facility in St. Louis where it could be analyzed fully before the decision was made whether to destroy the information permanently.

Jeff Brown sat forward, resting his face upon his clutched fists, watching anxiously for the first of what was expected to be several images flash upon his computer screen. They would initially appear as full screen photographs, then after a short twenty second delay, shrink to thumbnail images stacked along the left side of the screen. In this manner, he would have a quick look at what each image presented, but be able to select those images that offered better information for his intended use.

Finally, after an aggravating wait, the first of several images flashed in front of him and it didn't take his trained eye very much time to observe some disturbing information. By the third wide-field shot, he noticed the unmistakable image of a line of motor vehicles heading towards the south at a distance of about six kilometers from their position.

Clicking on a zoom image that most appealed to his inquisitive nature, he could see columns of Renault TRM 2000 light utility vehicles traveling at a slow, but consistent speed. He knew that this meant only one thing: Sudan was sending reinforcements to their southern border. *Why?*

He searched more intently through the images, desperately seeking answers to his most demanding question. *Where was Jennings?* Nowhere in any of the images was a trace of his lost team and another opportunity to seek them out wouldn't be available for some ninety minutes, a lifetime when a sizeable force was heading directly towards them.

"Trouble?" questioned John Mullen, the red haired member of his team who offered to search for the missing men.

"Yeah." Jeff made quick mental notes regarding the locations of the rapidly approaching convoy, and then quickly set about zipping the computer back into its case and inspecting his rifle magazine. "Big trouble."

"What's going on?" questioned the ever alert Ty Monroe as he nervously searched the horizon. "What the hell's going on?"

"Plenty." Jeff called over the fourth member of his team, Bill Graves, his most experienced associate, in order that he could lay out his instructions. "We've got bandits heading this way, about ten truck loads worth of the bastards. I don't know their intent. I don't know what they're armed with. I also don't know where Jennings' team is. They might've been taken."

"Oh dear, oh dear!" mumbled Ty quietly to himself.

"Relax." replied Graves, the stocky, bald man slightly tapping the butt of his rifle against the younger soldier's canteen, making a dull thump. "We have the advantage."

"What advantage?" barked Ty. "There's only *four* of us and there could be over a hundred of them!"

"Fair odds." retorted Graves as he calmly removed a package of chewing tobacco from his left shirt pocket, bit off a sizeable chunk, then replaced the packet into his shirt. He slowly chewed the wad in the left side of his mouth until its juices singed the back of his throat. "We can take 'em, if we need to."

"Nobody shoots until we have to." interjected Jeff Brown as he looked towards the known direction of the approaching convoy with the night vision goggles, scrutinizing the greenish horizon for any signs of movement. "Bill, spread everyone out."

Bill Graves quickly motioned for John Mullen to take the westernmost position, while he would take the eastern flank, about fifty meters bridging the gap between them. Ty Monroe would take position on the left side of the small embankment so that the newest member of their team could remain near Jeff Brown. Every man knew, however, that four people covering a line fifty meters in length was no match for a hundred or more hostiles.

The field of view within Brown's scope remained disturbingly bland – nothing but a surreal greenish hue. Even the land disappeared beyond a few tens of meters, leading to the belief that something might be amiss with the equipment. He knew better, however, and did not pay attention to anything save for that which would announce its presence from within the most greenish of colors.

The horizon is where the trouble would come from. From along the well-weathered path that barely registered as a road even in broad daylight. The same road that the earlier patrol had difficulty in navigating on foot. Should the expected convoy come down this particular path, he kept reasoning, it was for no other purpose than they knew that someone was here waiting for them.

His mind keep flowing back to the two kilometers that separated them from South Sudanese territory, and some semblance to legal protection. Here, they were far beyond such diplomacy and if found, could easily trigger events into a full-blown war between the two opposing nations.

Trying to remain focused on the search for the hostiles, Jeff had frequent second guesses as to whether he should've ordered a second pass of the satellite or send a more urgent appraisal to his superiors, all in an effort to communicate the situation should they be overtaken and eliminated.

He did not allow his facial expressions or his bodily movements betray this inner turmoil to his subordinates, merely glancing over into their general direction to ensure that each man remained at his post, silent and responsive. His small team had firepower, perhaps sufficient to destroy the convoy in whole, but much relied upon the element of surprise, and to a greater extent, quiet extraction south of the border.

Jeff Brown's orders were straightforward. Should he and his team be compromised, then they were to pull back behind the border as rapidly as possible so that no evidence of their existence remained in hostile territory. This, he knew, may have already been sacrificed if Chet Jennings' team had been nabbed.

The monochrome greenish image of the night vision scope grew tiresome, and he frequently lowered the instrument so that he could scan the horizon with his unaided eyes, an action more for comfort than operational security. Jeff simply wanted to observe *something* – anything that would answer his primary question of what they were going up against.

Seconds felt like minutes, minutes felt like hours. He thought that he could hear Ty Monroe's heartbeat racing across the air until he realized that it was his own, rhythmically calling out the time. Still, nothing. Not a damn thing showed either in his scope or visually upon the horizon. *Where are they?*

Before he had time to reflect upon his thoughts, a tiny speck of light appeared in the center of his scope's field of view and quickly metamorphosed into a brilliant orb of luminosity. Seconds later, a powerful shockwave blasted over their tiny encampment and shook the dust off of everything and everyone present.

Someone yelled an expletive in a voice that sounded disturbingly familiar and Jeff dragged himself back up to the edge of the bulge where his unaided eyes witnessed a towering fireball that ascended at an unknown distance. The explosion had been close, as a quick mental calculation of the time lag between light and sound showed, but it was still beyond their horizon and nothing was illuminated by the slowly fading ball of light, particularly any people near enough to cause them harm.

Jeff knew instinctively that he had a decision to make regarding obeying his orders to the letter by remaining there until they were discovered or heading south now and avoiding detection by the hordes of hostile forces that he knew would be coming to investigate matters. He chose the latter.

"We're bugging out!" called Jeff Brown as he grabbed his equipment. "Mullen, take the point. Graves follow up the rear and let me know if you spy *anything!*"

"Check." answered Graves as he turned his attention towards the northern horizon to cover his teams exit.

"Right!" replied John Mullen, who'd instinctively began scouting the southern egress route that had been identified within their pre-mission briefing.

Jeff watched as Mullen's silhouette disappeared down a small gully before gently nudging Ty Monroe to follow him. Behind them, in the distance, he could hear secondary rumblings indicating that whatever exploded initially was still active. The fact that something blew up hinted at the presence of another team, most probably Chet Jennings or at least elements of his team, but Jeff didn't permit his hopes to rise too high for if it were his friend's team, they were in a very nasty situation.

Within minutes, the four-man group was tracing a pre-determined path across the African plain, stopping frequently to check for detection, then resuming their southward movements. They moved quickly, but with panther-like precision, no wasted efforts, no unnecessary sounds.

Jeff knew that he had to, at a minimum, acknowledge their withdrawal from the forward camp and chose to send a quick code from his satellite telephone – the numbers 427 indicating that *four* men were traveling *to* the *south* and hoped against all odds that another such message had been received coming from Jennings.

The trip south took nearly an hour and a half, owing to the selective motions of a group trying to remain undetected. Each member found new vigor with the opportunity to actually move in an upright position, the first such opportunity in nearly two weeks. Young Monroe, especially, relished in the delight of finally moving away from hostile territory, an action more in characteristic with his dash and snatch experience.

Regardless, each teammate moved away from their encampment with a heavy heart, personally feeling the absence of Chet Jennings, Carl Northrop, Harlan "Vince" Vingassi, and Bob Ventura. Each, in their own way, silently offered a prayer that their friends were safe somewhere, perhaps already well behind friendly lines and waiting for them while sitting back idle, downing a cool one, and regaling all present with stories on their miraculous escape from the north.

8

JASON LEANED FORWARD and rested his hands on the edge of the steel desk as he stared at the images flickering past on the Silicon Graphics computer screen. "Dammit! What the hell is going on there?"

"I don't know, Sir." replied the operator, hurriedly trying to enhance the photographs. "It was an explosion of some sort, but it will be another hour and a half before the satellite returns to the area, and then it will be slightly off target."

Jack Stephens stood in the corner of the room, balancing a stack of transcripts pinned underneath his chin as he tore through the messages. "Team Alpha One Seven called for the development of aerial recon." He lifted his chin, allowing the papers to drop into his hands. "Then someone sent word that four men were heading south, apparently right after the first explosion."

Jason rocked back on his feet but still hung fast to the desk. "What about Alpha One Eight?"

"Not a word." Jack tossed the stack of messages onto a file tray, a few of the papers scattered about as they flew into the current of a nearby fan. "And it was Jeff Brown that had ordered the satellite recon."

"Is he a good man?"

"I consider him to be the best."

"What about Chester Jennings?"

"I consider Chet.. I consider *all* of my men to be the best in the business."

Jason nodded quietly, finally loosening his grip on the desk as he walked over to a water cooler and indulged himself with a long drink before crumbling the paper cup in a fit of frustration. "Damn, I wish that we did have an aerial recon capability."

"We do." sighed Jack reflectively. "But it's been delayed in deployment for a couple of months as we work out some control glitches."

Jason threw his friend an overt sneer of frustration. "Had I known that I would've recommended a delay in launching our operations."

"Wouldn't have mattered." reassured Jack. "We were already in the area and have been running recon patrols north of the border for some six months now."

"Still, I don't like sending men anywhere without the best available equipment."

Jack couldn't argue with the sentiment, but he also knew that they would always be operating without *something* that would make life a little easier. Hell, they were already spending nearly a hundred million a year in project developments alone and with their fiscal efficiency, they already had programs in place that were the envy of U.S. military forces.

"Listen, Jack." Jason calmed himself with a few quick breaths, then walked over to where his friend stood. "I don't want our efforts to remain hodgepodge. I want to develop the best systems, the best techniques, the best personnel on the planet. Nothing else will suffice."

Stephens nodded, mentally going over how many hundreds of millions more it would cost to develop the kind of military force that Jason had hoped for. *Was it practical?*

"I know what you're thinking." answered Jason. "If we don't commit every resource at our disposal, then we can't expect people to take our mission seriously. Hell, even the politicians will support an action if it serves their purpose. We must stand against the world like a steel saber ready to swipe at evil wherever and whenever we find it. If we don't believe this, then we'd better quit now."

"Don't forget." replied Jack. "I can't sacrifice Jamie's family empire just for my own purposes."

"Then every business that we create from now on will serve this purpose. Agreed?"

"Every business that we create for *this* purpose."

Jason nodded so that he wouldn't have to answer verbally. He wanted all resources diverted to his master plan and knew that Jack's businesses were of strategic importance. He also knew, however, that it wouldn't be appropriate to involve the heretofore diplomatic *Mrs.* Stephens anymore than he would've expected Samantha to partake in his own global adventures.

"Then we'll simply have to make our efforts self-supporting." Jason spoke as a matter of fact. "Our organization will have to earn its own keep, pay for its own products, and maintain its own budget."

"Oh?" It was a statement that Jack had theorized about before, but had since eliminated because he knew it would defeat their mission before it even began.

"Yes. We must find a way to make our efforts earn their keep." He calmly walked over in front of Jack and studied his facial expressions before continuing. "I know that it's virtually impossible to rationalize, but what happens when we're gone? I'm not doing this for my benefit. Hell, my life ended thirteen years ago as far as I consider it. I want to accomplish our goals for future humanity, so that our species can survive long enough to make it off of this damn planet and colonize other worlds. Only then, can humans endure until the end of the time."

Jack knew that Jason was right, if not wholly practical. Whether or not the human species was to continue depended solely upon whether it could get off of the planet. This was not theological revelation anymore than it was mystical fiction, it was basic scientific reality. However, to plan eons into the future seemed hardly appropriate when they had one lost team in Africa and were on the verge of getting their asses handed to them by a hostile nation intent on proving to the world that some evil Americans were tampering in regional politics.

"First things, first." Jason returned to the computer console where he had earlier watched the events unfold before them. "We take care of matters in Africa, stabilize the region, and then work on saving the planet."

"Agreed." Jack stopped to retrieve the communications notes that had been blowing around by the fan. "For now, let's find out what the hell blew up north of the border. We know that it was a line of French-made trucks, now let's determine what was on those vehicles."

"Preliminary analysis shows that it was petroleum or a petroleum product." replied the computer operator, scanning over the broad spectrum data. "*SkyAction IV* snapped a shot as it passed over Tanzania. Preliminary spectrometer readings indicate that it was a refined product of some sort, probably diesel or gasoline. The bird was too far away at the time for a definite."

"Do we have anything in the area that can give us a definite?" asked Jason, observing the images over the shoulder of the operator. "What about an aircraft?"

"It'd be risky." replied Jack.

Jason thought over the actions, placing his hand gently on the computer operator's shoulder. "Direct a C-130 to fly over the site. Call it a navigational oversight, a humanitarian effort, whatever. Just have them video everything they can and get the hell back into friendly territory."

"Yes, sir."

Jack walked over to a first aid kit and removed a couple of Tylenol® caplets from a small package, then headed over to the water cooler to fill a cup. "We're pushing it. They'll have everybody they can descending down on that area. "He quickly swallowed the pills, washing them down with a sizeable gulp of water that nearly went down the wrong tube. "They might think that our aircraft had something to do with the explosions."

"We need to know." was Jason's only answer.

"Hell, maybe they'll even locate our lost team."

The last sentiment played heavily on Jason's mind. He always hated losing any of his people, even if they were a simple janitor who retired from one of his plants. The prospect of people under his care *dying* drove home the reality that his activities weren't simply commercial enterprises.

It was one thing for evil people to die, it was another thing when a good person died, and all of Jason's people were good. He made sure of that. Still, reflecting upon his wife's agonizing death, he realized that in life, good people often die and often die horribly.

"We have an aircraft coming in." The computer operator broke the silence. "C-130 that will be passing over the target area in....five...make that six minutes."

"Do they have video available?" asked Jack.

"That's a negative, but they do have a digital camera and can send us pictures via satellite link."

Jason quickly glanced at his wristwatch. "At least we'll have some answers."

Strangely, the six minutes seemed to fly by for the two anxious men standing quietly within the vessel's command center. It was ten minutes before the first, grainy image appeared on the computer screen showing a burning line of wreckage that used to be vehicles. Do to the darkness, the quality of the image was poor, but they could see that the vehicles were stopped in their tracks, overtaken by whatever caused the explosion or explosions.

The second image was clearer, but showed no further details than had the first, save for an unmistakable view of several soldiers raising their weapons *towards the camera*.

"Get that damn plane out of there!" ordered Jack.

"Already in South Sudanese territory." replied the operator calmly. "Should be landing in about ten minutes."

"Keep all forces along the border on alert." added Jason. "We're in hot territory now."

"Have the crew debriefed fully, they may have seen something that wouldn't show up on camera." Jack motioned for Jason to follow him into the passageway.

THE TWO MEN had spent an hour discussing the formation of their new organization with Jack bringing up the historical background on the Gatestrian Knights.

"An interesting concept," agreed Jason, contemplating the organization as a basis for copy. "But aren't you afraid that someone will compare us with the Nazis of the Second World War? They were fanatics on this type of thing and misused the history of the Templar Knights, for one."

"Perhaps." conceded Jack. "But the Gatestrian Knights are largely unknown, if they existed at all. I think, however, that we could divert attention by offering comparisons with the Knights of Columbus, for example."

Jason nodded in agreement but knew they were still trending on semantics. "Yet, the KofC doesn't conduct military operations throughout the world."

"Listen, we're always going to be misunderstood." Jack removed his eyeglasses momentarily to rub away the sting from the salt air that infiltrated the ship's library through an open porthole. "Do we judge ourselves by the judgment of others? Or do we judge ourselves by how much we accomplish of what we believe in?"

"I say, screw everyone else."

"Good."

Jason outlined the code of conduct that the *new* Gatestrian Knights should obey, such as the total respect for innocent lives, especially that of women and infants. He stressed the need to protect the Catholic Church and its policies from all adversaries, in particular those who try to destroy it from within. Finally, he mentioned the need to feed, educate, provide health care, and employ persons of faith all over the world.

Jack agreed in principle, adding that the new organization should function along the moral conditions common during the thirteenth century, but with the caveat that they use twenty-first century technology to hit, and hit *hard* those organizations and individuals who seemed determined to destroy innocent human lives as they saw fit.

"In other words.." continued Jason. "..We use force to influence our agenda on the world."

Jack's stomach soured at the mention of the word *agenda* with its primarily liberal connotation. "I'd rather mention that we're a military force outright and shy away from the use of political terms. We're in this for the long haul and we shouldn't handcuff ourselves with concern for what others may think or characterize us as."

"Explain."

"Listen, the world evolves either through migration or military conquest, and we're through migrating on earth so there's nowhere to go except up. That brings us to the basic reality of military conquest. Alexander the Great, the Roman Empire, centuries of Chinese history, the New World — all examples of human evolution by conquest. Don't think that it works? Just ask the mayor of Hiroshima or Nagasaki. Perhaps Dresden? People listen when they have to listen, so we set about *making* them listen. We use every ordnance at our disposal, attack at enemies at every location they're found, and achieve every goal that we set about for ourselves."

"Wow." Jason was taken back slightly by the forthrightness of his friend. "I'm glad that you're on my side."

"Listen, Jace. I just don't want to fuck up our operation like the West usually does. Consider Europe. Once a world class civilization, now a bunch of pussies crying about being left out of history. Even the United States can't act as it should because every action has to be given the green light by Congress. Now, *there's* a bunch of goddamn bastards."

"Conquest without conscience." marveled Jason as he walked over to the open porthole to gaze out across the sea.

"Conquest *with* conscience." retorted Jack. "We don't indiscriminately kill, but we don't use precision so effectively as not to punish those who know better."

"I'm not quite certain that I follow you."

"Listen, Jason. Ever wonder why wars seem to take forever to end nowadays? We're too precise; we don't let those who place the bastards who are in power know that their actions – or inactions, for that matter – require responsibility. Again, I say look at Japan or Germany in World War II. We annihilated those countries so bad the locals had no option but to develop democracies from scratch. They were the idiots who allowed Hitler and Tojo to climb in power. Today, the West's weapons are so precise that people are no longer *part* of war and if you're not affected by war, you won't do anything to end it."

Jason began to see Jack's point. Nobody worried about crime until they were robbed. "The world *is* too sanitary, too desensitized."

"More than that. Whenever a terrorist blows up somebody, the world's press makes it sound like they were abused, driven to poverty, or somehow neglected. Yet, when America defends itself, the media make our nation out to be the bad guys."

"So do we punish everyone, including the media and the press?"

"Why the hell not?" Jack thought out loud, deciding for a moment to throw caution into the wind. "Are they not responsible for what they do? Should we allow them to cause casualties by errant or, worse, fraudulent reporting? Is being a journalist somehow indicative of being given a free rein to do whatever you damn well please?"

"Then what separates us from the bad guys?"

"Jesus Christ, Jason! Who terrorizes the terrorists? Who deposes the despots? The *people* for cryin' out loud? Shit, before they do anything, hundreds of thousands of innocents die and then only if the country in question is within a politically attractive area. What sets us different from those bastards is that we don't target innocent lives. Listen, we must do what is *right* not what is popular."

Jack had given Jason a lot to think about. The moral implications of what he had stated were tremendous, but he also made a valuable point regarding the failure to carry out these actions. "Aren't we supposed to turn the other cheek?"

"You slap me, I'll turn the other cheek. You try to saw my leg off and I'll flatten you like you were yesterday's pizza. Get the picture?"

"Yes, I think that I do." Jason remembered the conversation from earlier. "Why then, were you afraid to commit all of your resources to this mission?"

"Simply because I have a wife and child and these people are going to become mad as hell at us and I'd rather not be openly involved in this mission. But only for Jamie and Jonathon's sake."

"Point taken."

Jack departed to relieve himself in the ship's head, leaving Jason alone to contemplate what they had been discussing. He was now beginning to formulate the Gatestrian Knights as an organization that would protect the innocent by stepping beyond the boundaries of international law in order to punish those who caused great harm. It was a significant step beyond that which he had been planning, but a logical extension to the mission as it could only be adopted.

To meld the characteristics of medieval Christianity, combat akin to that exercised by ancient Ninjas, and modern technology seemed to epitomize the tasks that they had set about for themselves. Whether or not it was capable of being done, remained to be seen, but Jason never lost a battle with ambition and he knew deep down in his heart that this would succeed also.

9

CHET JENNINGS HAD a decision to make. The tall, lanky ex-Army Ranger captain stood in the shadow of several burning Renaults watching over dozens of Sudanese and Arab prisoners for which he and his team had just become responsible. Alpha One Eight was now knee deep in a quagmire of international proportions. If they released the prisoners they would in effect announce to the entire planet that the Americans were operating *in* Sudanese territory. On the other hand, if they took the prisoners south with them – a tricky situation being that they were outnumbered to begin with – then they could be regarded as kidnappers.

The luxury of deferring to higher authority was destroyed along with the team's radio, itself a casualty of a hail of automatic fire that erupted when Alpha One Eight was serendipitously uncovered by the Sudanese.

Jennings remained silent, counting the prisoners in his mind as he sought out solutions to his predicament before reinforcements began to pour in from the north. They numbered thirty-six, far more than he considered manageable, but even a single individual could topple the whole operation before it even began.

The team's second in command, Carl Northrop, cautiously moved closer to Jennings, his attention never wavering very far from the group of hostiles under his direct care. "Chet, we can't take these guys with us."

"We can't leave them behind either." replied Jennings.

"Guess we're screwed." Northrop moved back towards the prisoners, frequently glancing up towards the sky, wondering whether any more aircraft would be flying overhead.

Chet Jennings had been wondering about that too. They heard an airplane, a *large* airplane make a quick pass several minutes earlier, but could not ascertain as to whom it belonged. The consensus was that it was friendly, but they couldn't be certain. Nothing could be certain given the unfolding of events in this godforsaken place.

One thing Jennings could be sure of, however, was that as soon as the blast filled the night sky, Jeff Brown's group would've had no alternative but to head back down south. He would've done the same, but now realized that they couldn't even expect the other four men to show up and assist them.

He also knew that time was running out and running out fast. Whether for good or bad, a decision had to be made *now*. "Throw the Sudanese weapons into the fire!"

"Right!" called out Vince Vingassi, an energetic if somewhat seasoned veteran of the team as he began chucking AK-47s and APG launchers into the blaze as if he were stoking the fires of some aged iron horse. Ammunition was thrown into a nearby ditch, unusable without the weapons for which they were designed.

Carl Northrop along with the final member of the team, Bob Ventura, began herding the terrified prisoners into a tight group, intentionally keeping them away from the weapons cache which could prove fatal in their mismatched situation.

The roaring fire, fueled by countless steel drums of gasoline, made quick work of the weapons, but it was the gasoline itself that caused much concern for Jennings. The fuel obviously was intended to be pre-positioned for vehicles that were yet to come. This meant only one thing: reinforcements.

He looked over his map, knowing that the inbound convoy could only come from the north or the northeast. He decided, therefore, to send the prisoners on a march to the northwest. First, however, he ordered them to strip to their shorts in order to prevent them from concealing any weapons or give them thoughts of carrying out any action besides heading further back into their homeland.

"Carl, you and Vince make sure those guys keep heading straight before you double back."

"Right!" replied Carl Northrop, knowing instinctively that he had just been informed that the team was splitting up, at least for the moment.

Jennings had no choice. If he pulled back using the honor system, the prisoners could've attacked them. Thirty-six unarmed men could easily overwhelm four who were. By having them move under guard, perhaps they could successfully thwart any attempt at rebellion. He also hoped that the prisoners would be more inclined to hightail for safety than to risk their lives, especially if they weren't threatened with the ominous presence of all four guards.

It was a calculated risk, but the only one that could've been made in a matter of seconds, the very nature of combat decision making. To prolong debate on the issue would've placed everyone, both friend and foe, into severe jeopardy.

As Jennings and Bob Ventura slowly watched the large group head off into the distance, they remained for several minutes before turning towards the south. However, their departure was abruptly halted by a chance, most gruesome discovery.

"Chet!" Ventura froze in his tracks, his face sullen and pale, a feature easily discernible even in the darkness of the night.

Jennings had started to inquire as to what had caused his soldier so much trauma, but before he could get even a word out, he saw it for himself. Dangling from one of the few intact vehicles – the third from the front of the convoy – was a small, worn duffle bag. Protruding from the bag, incomprehensible in its viciousness, was the bound bodies of at least two infants.

Moving slowly towards the bag, fearing that his mind was playing tricks on him, Jennings lifted the opening of the duffle with his rife and bodies of numerous infants slid out and hit the African earth with a nauseating plop. He spun around in horror, his teammate acknowledging the confirmation, and fought tears from building up within his eyes.

Without the need for a long observation, he could tell that the babies were bound, two or three together, with their throats slit and bodies mutilated. Leaning against the side of the truck for support, he peered inside to see several more bags, undoubtedly containing more bodies and fell backwards in utter disbelief.

Neither man spoke; they didn't need to express a word. Gazing out towards the horizon where the prisoners were being led, ultimately, to their freedom they realized that the fuel laden trucks were not meant to service an inbound convoy, they were to serve as a funeral pyre, a devastating example of humanity at its worst.

Almost immediately, Chet Jennings realized that the purpose of the heinous crime more than likely was to instigate trouble between the two Sudanese nations. It didn't take a further leap of the imagination to figure that the South Sudanese, mostly Christians in faith, would probably be blamed for the murders.

With a quick pointing motion of his hand, Jennings instructed Bob Ventura that they were now heading towards the line of prisoners somewhere beyond the horizon. They would stop the group, take command of them, and bring them back to the crime scene to receive punishment or some other form of retribution that Jennings had not, at the present, clarity of mind to consider.

The two soldiers moved overtly, just short of a jog as they pushed ahead irrespective of whatever or whomever they came across. Their haste served two purposes. First, they wanted to intercept the group before hostile reinforcements could reach them. Second, they wanted to stop Northrop and Vingassi from releasing the prisoners to their own care or, worse, possibly falling into a trap and coming under harm themselves.

After about seven minutes of quick movement, Jennings saw the outline of a large group of men a hundred yards in front of their position. "Stop!" he called out, searching frantically for his men. "Get them stopped! Now!"

"Chet?" came a confused voice out of the darkness.

"Don't let those bastards move!" yelled Jennings, the pretense of operational covertness being thrown out a long time ago. "Get them down on their knees!"

After a few more minutes of charging ahead, his rifle aimed squarely at the mass of partially nude men, Jennings reached the point where Carl Northrop stood but ignored his second officer and ran through the crowd until he spied an Arab individual that he had earlier assumed was the leader of the ragtag mob.

Jennings, short of breath, grabbed the pudgy man by the shoulder, yanking him out of the line of men that mumbled in confusion. "*Hal tatakallam Ingliizi?*"

"*La.*" The man lied.

"Bullshit!" snapped Jennings as he threw the man down on the ground hard. "Carl, shoot this fucker!"

"No! No!" exclaimed the man in terror, quickly crawling across the ground before he finally had the composure needed to regain his footing, more bouncing his body up than lifting with his feet. "I speak English! I speak English!"

Carl Northrop had raised his rifle to carry out the order, if somewhat confused as to its purpose and still not wholly contemplating the turn of events that unfolded within the past couple of minutes. "Shit, the bastard *does* speak English."

Jennings ignored Northrop and focused his attention directly on the individual that now stood in front of him, shaking profusely. "You have only one chance to live, and that's to answer my questions truthfully. Do you understand?"

"Yes. Yes."

"Who murdered those babies on the trucks?"

Both Carl's and Vince's faces turned deadly pale, then flushed with anger as the realization of what was transpiring before them took hold, but the individual being interrogated remained quiet, gaining in both composure and confidence.

"Who murdered those babies!" repeated Jennings, his eyes swelling with ferocity, an expression that could be discerned from several meters away. "Answer me or so help me I'll blow away the fuckin' lot of you now!"

"We do not know." The man mumbled, barely audible and it became clear that he wasn't privy to all that had happened. "What babies?"

Jennings debated forcing the man to speak, but concluded that it was fruitless either because the man didn't know about the bodies or probably wouldn't tell the truth if he had known, given the amount of time with which they had to interrogate him.

Calling the other four members of his team together, he told Northrop and Vingassi what had been discovered on the trucks and that they would more than likely be required to escort the prisoners back into South Sudan. He also mentioned his belief that regardless of the situation, they were probably in for a tremendous amount of trouble because few would believe the discovery owing to the fact that their team was illegally operating in a sovereign nation's territory.

"We will photograph the bodies." instructed Jennings, motioning for Ventura to check the status of the team's video camera. "Then have these bastards bury them. Once we're back across the border, we'll make contact with Tango Echo Deuce and judge our future actions accordingly."

The other men nodded in agreement, Ventura trying to avoid the thought of having to photograph the mutilated corpses, a spectacle that he had no desire to witness again.

"Babies?" questioned Northrop as he walked over towards Jennings.

Jennings nodded, but said nothing. The tears swelling up within his eyes spoke volumes.

In a fit of rage, Northrop turned around and struck the Arab leader's face with the butt of his rifle, fracturing his left jawbone and sending a torrent of teeth and blood onto the ground below. "You bastard!"

"Northrop!" commanded Jennings as he grabbed his subordinate by the collar. "We need these guys alive and in good shape!"

Jennings turned towards the prisoners and separated the Arabs from the Africans, and instructed them that he was going to move them to South Sudan for medical assistance and interrogation. Whether or not they were to be released, he mentioned, depended upon whether they cooperated with any investigation regarding the horrendous murder of the children.

With him, Ventura, and Northrop serving as guards, Jennings had Vingassi strap the prisoners together in pairs to allow for better management. Then, with a point of his rifle, the group began the slow, awkward march towards where the smoldering trucks still illuminated the night.

It took about half an hour for the tired and sore train of prisoners and attendant guards to reach the location where Chet Jennings immediately set six of the prisoners free in order to bury the dead.

To avoid corrupting evidence, he had the dead infants buried as they were, but arranged the graves in neat lines, allowing all who may photograph the site via satellite or aircraft to know that these were in fact graves. Then, when all fifty seven graves were dug, filled, and covered, he had the six exceptionally tired prisoners tied back up and the party again made its way toward the south.

By this time, the sun had already begun to blaze down upon the African plain, but neither Jennings nor his men cared much about concealment. On the contrary, they hoped that the entire world would learn of the tragic events that took place on this little spot of land in a tiny new nation isolated within the planet's oldest surviving continent.

As Jennings walked towards the South Sudanese border, his head hung low with disgust, his body sore with anger and exhaustion. Part of him wanted to shoot every one of the prisoners for what they had done, but also knew that they might've only been pawns. His was a position where such decisions weren't made. He just wanted to bring the witnesses into camp so that justice, in whatever form, could be served.

10

THE SHINY, ALL-BLACK Boeing 777-300ER executive aircraft banked to the north high above Kenya and headed into South Sudanese airspace over the Eastern Equatorial Province and began the ever so slow decent that would terminate at the newly constructed private airport near the town of Rumbek, after an uneventful flight from London, itself a routine stopover from its origin at Orlando International.

Jason shifted his sore body within the plush leather seat in order to get a view of the Sudano-Guinean savanna that sprawled out far below, marveling at the contradiction of sights. The one, a luxurious twin-jet with a smoke gray and imported cherry wood interior, complete with Sony large screen television, master bedroom and marble bath, conference center with satellite communications capability and, for the stressed out corporate executive, a fully stocked wet bar. The other, an ancient plain teeming with Addra and Dorcas Gazelle, a host of Zebra, Elano, Black Rhino, Red Flanked Duiker, and nearly one million White-Eared Kob.

His ears began to pop, muffling all sounds as he felt a slight drop in the altitude of the aircraft, but returned his attention to the folder that sat upon his lap. The leather-bound portfolio contained a description of the wreckage where dozens of mutilated bodies were found, a post-mission debriefing from Team Alpha One Eight, and several newspaper reports regarding the alleged atrocities.

It was these last items that deeply disturbed Jason. *Alleged atrocities*? He saw the photographs. He read the reports. He also knew his men. How could anyone not believe that something horrible had happened along the road south from Babanūsah?

The sun shone through the side window, reflected off of the papers that he held in his hands and blazed into his eyes, forcing Jason to glance away, but the image stayed burned within his mind. It was as if God Himself was illuminating the event, shining His light upon the very facts that the rest of the world chose to remain dark about.

Placing the papers back into the folder, Jason couldn't bear anymore. He had long accepted death within his life, even cruel death, but this was something far beyond cruelty, it was downright heinous. The murder of dozens of children could not be justified through any explanation imaginable by mortal man and yet here was the international media questioning even the very existence of the fact!

"Sir, we will be landing in about twenty minutes." spoke an attractive blond, dressed smartly in a navy blue flight attendant's uniform before she left to inform Jason's on board security team which occupied the rear of the cabin.

"Thank you." Jason wondered whether she had any inkling as to why he had hastily arranged the trip. Sure, everybody knew of his exploits, but this was definitely a different operation altogether.

He looked towards the group of men chatting in the back who, like him, had swapped their pristine business suits for khaki trousers and shirts. Everyone was professional. Everyone did their job. *Did anyone ever show any emotions?*

Jason found it difficult to contemplate doing his job without constantly considering the implications. His team, however, were strict professionals who did what was needed to be done. Hell, even the flight attendants seemed to move according to some predestined plan, a well-orchestrated and choreographed script that seem to belie their human nature.

He felt himself lose weight rapidly; an indication that the plane's descent was increasing, and calmly straightened up his seat, before lowering the window shade. This was to be a brief trip – if all went well – and he hoped that he could get out of the area soon, before he himself became front page news. Undue publicity now would surely ruin the chances that anything that he and Jack would do in the future could be done in their trademarked silence.

As much as Jason loved traveling and exploring new cultures, he felt wholly uncomfortable with the formalities involved with travel. It was an ironic twist of fate that hounded him that, now that he could afford to travel at will, he never could venture anywhere without massive security precautions, advance teams on the ground beforehand and, much to his dismay, the absence of his beloved confidant, Samantha.

He was alone in a sea of people, he thought to himself as he watched the security men stationed in the rear of the cabin busily inspecting their side arms and automatic rifles prior to landing. Everyone around him was *paid* to behave the way that they did. Money, he was well aware, could become the most fleeting of loyalties.

Fortunately money did have advantages. His flight, for example, had already been cleared by the South Sudanese Customs & Immigration Authority, a fact that rested along the same lines as the knowledge that money was the only instrument sharp enough to lay waste to the miles of red tape that any bureaucracy could conjure up.

Money bred power and power bred action. What set Jason apart from the rest of the crowd was that he focused his action upon a narrowly defined field of battle. He surged ahead in his activities and rarely, if ever, pondered their failures for more than a few quiet moments of reflection such as now.

He also realized that he was now embarking upon a totally new direction, far beyond the heroics of rescuing captives or returning exiles to their former homes. What lay ahead was decidedly diplomatic, almost national in nature. By allowing himself to take a direct role in Jack Stephens' South Sudan stepchild, he was now committing his operations to a *fixed* plot of land, a piece of real estate that was both defined and *targetable*.

What this meant, precisely, was that his troops not only had to defend a belief system, they now had to defend a nation. This was new territory for him and he didn't know if merely having money was adequate enough for the job. Jason knew history; there were plenty of people with money – actors, rock stars, supermodels, for example — who totally destroyed nations by butting their heads in where they didn't belong.

His case was different, he kept reminding himself, because those examples had no practical experience in creating anything save for their own inflated egos and interpretations of art. Jason, on the other hand, had created businesses and organizations which had to function according to standardized policies and procedures. No, Jason Task wasn't simply an idealistic activist.

"We will be landing at Paradise Field in approximately five minutes." The pilot's voice over the intercom seemed uncharacteristically nonchalant, Jason thought, for the time and place of their destination. "Will the flight attendants please prepare for landing."

Paradise Field, named for its location, as it was very reminiscent of the equatorial plains of East Africa where science dictates that man first arose, was a newly constructed airport that consisted largely of a solitary runway flanked by a series of concrete buildings housing support personnel, communications centers, and medical facilities. For all of its appearance, one could expect to see a herd of buffalo ranging towards the many swamps that surrounded the area.

What the airport lacked in aesthetics, it made up for in functionality. Its long runway took in the consistent flights of Lockheed C-130Js that poured in equipment, personnel, and supplies that shored up Jack Stephens' host of activities that dominated the agenda of the current South Sudanese government.

Whereas there was no strict schedule of inbound flights – for obvious security reasons – there was an abnormally large gap today as the runway was laid bare for the approaching black luxury aircraft. In the distance, militarized Sikorsky S-76 helicopters swarmed over the perimeter, searching for unauthorized personnel.

No sooner than the big, black aircraft had landed than a series of brown and tan Land Rovers raced out to meet the jet, disgorging a number of security personnel who quickly formed a protective corridor around the airliner. Shortly thereafter, a ramp was driven out to the plane so that its occupants could disembark and the aircraft itself towed to a secured hanger for servicing.

JASON DISPENSED WITH the formalities; he wanted to get right down to the fundamentals.

"Do we know who committed these atrocities?" he spoke, selecting a prominent chair within the brightly lit conference room.

A tall, rugged individual full of military bearing and composure walked up to the front of the room and spoke with a distinctively Southern drawl. "We believe that it was forces loyal to General Abu Nasir Kuraymahiyyun who, as you may be aware, overthrew the so-called legitimate government last year. We don't know much about the General, and we're not exactly sure of his true name – nobody is – but everyone knows him as *iilahhaam*. The Butcher."

"Is this the same mysterious bastard who's hellbent on destroying the whole damn continent?" questioned Jason as he leaned forward, resting his arms on his knees. He was well aware of the chaotic situation in Sudan as a whole, and the shaky situation within this part of the world may very well work to his advantage.

"Yes, sir." replied the speaker. "As far as we know, and this is a problem as nobody is really certain of a lot of things that have happened over the course of the past year, the General has a firm grip on the country and has executed hundreds of people. Arabs, Muslims, Christians, his brother-in-law, you name it. This guy doesn't have too many friends, I'm afraid."

"Then *why* is this guy even in power?"

"Well, Mr. Task. The same ageless reasons. Brutality, a local population in fear, and many who simply support him because he pushes hope down their throats. It could be a number of things, but the underlying reason that he's *still* in power is that the rest of the world is too preoccupied with events elsewhere."

Jason leaned backwards, rocking slightly in his chair as it squeaked slightly, catching the attention of all within the room. "Is he supported by the Islamists?"

"The extremists, I would say." replied the speaker. "Anyone who hates the West and democracy, he'd find a use for even if they hated him personally."

"Please continue."

Jason listened attentively to the speaker who described the mayhem that followed the coup in the north, about how the Sudanese army, led by the infamous Butcher, brutally overthrew the Sudanese government, which itself wasn't exactly the darling of the international community.

He heard about efforts to promote terrorism worldwide, the fallacious promotion of radical fundamentalism, and the attempted procurement of deadly weapons. The picture that unfolded before Jason was that of a madman, but only the latest in a long line of dictators who went about their work largely unnoticed by the world until it was far too late, and sometimes not even then.

He found that he needn't really listen to the speaker for the story rang all too familiar. It was a story of salvation by tyranny, a local populace that had inadvertently allowed a psychotic ruler to come into power through the diversion afforded by social welfare and injustice. During the 1930's, for example, this same level of incredulous idiocy paved the way for the likes of Adolf Hitler and Benito Mussolini to name but only two.

Still, Jason knew that economic distress or even the mere thought of it was a powerful reason for otherwise rational human beings to forfeit sound judgment and sacrifice their nation's future. During 1992, for example, the United States itself elected Bill Clinton into office, ultimately for two terms, a move that seriously jeopardized the country's military forces just prior to its thrust into the most intense era of conflict that it had ever witnessed, all on the theory that a visibly strong economy was far better than a factually sound defense.

He was well aware of the 'herd mentality' that most people, regardless of culture, were naturally drawn to. Whether they lived in downtown Detroit or suburban Khartoum, people just wanted to wake up, eat, breathe, and go to bed. Most knew, fortunately, that this level of existence required some form of effort on their part, namely the action otherwise known as hard work.

Still, concern for the outside and, in particular, the future, rarely worked its way into this daily routine. So, when someone came along breathing fire and spouting tales of narcissistic glory, they occasionally abandoned the monotony of their existence and fell for the bullshit hook, line, and sinker.

All human beings were subject to this distraction as witnessed by the popularity of science fiction epics that regularly captured the attention of the movie going public. Jason knew this, knew that inside of every person on the planet was a longing for something more powerful and glorious than themselves.

Whether this intoxicating demand for excitement was fueled by religion, sports, entertainment, or the unabashed support for someone who may very well demand their life in payment, depended solely upon the individual in question.

Jason fidgeted in his chair as he realized that with over six billion people on this planet, there were plenty of idiots for every category. With this reality in mind, he no longer considered the question of *why* some people came into power, merely what to do with them once they had.

"Do we have sufficient resources at our disposal to remove this so-called Butcher from power?" Jason's question caught the entire room off guard, many of those present throwing incredulous looks in his direction so he repeated the question. "Can we do something about the military controlling the northern government?"

"Soon, perhaps." replied a rather tall individual crowned with a silvery bushel of hair, puffing on a stogie that was nearly as long as his cane. "We have the capability, but not the materiel. At least, not yet."

"Then how soon?" Jason knew that something had to be done to avoid future atrocities.

"Three weeks."

Jason nodded in acknowledgement, then turned towards one of the advisors that had been posted to assist him onsite. "Mr. Kent, describe our situation with the media coverage of this event."

"Well, Mr. Task." The dark-haired man with a childish face stood up to address the crowd, his British accent setting his nationality apart from the rest of the group. "Most of the media organizations have reported this atrocity with those leaning towards more conservative views referring to it as a travesty and those leaning towards liberal calling it as something that should be merely investigated. No one wants to deny that it is horrendous, just that they don't want to point fingers until the results of an investigation are in."

"Which could take months?"

"Yes, if properly done. Most of the European press want a lengthy investigation..."

"Naturally."

"... a lengthy investigation conducted by a blue ribbon panel."

"What about the Americans?"

"The United States is split between those who mimic the European position and those who want to address some form of military response. The same kind of talk that led up to the invasion of Iraq several years ago."

"If we chose to move against the north." Jason asked. "What will the response be from this government and the rest of the world for that matter?"

"The South Sudanese government wouldn't like it. President Baroque-Zambi would probably be terrified unless we had *overwhelming* power at our disposal. As for the rest of the world, well, you know that they will characterize us as inflammatory warmongers or something akin to this."

Jason walked around the room, contemplating the options that were available. After a few casual circuits of the room, he approached the front. "Gentlemen, I am not a diplomat. Neither am I a military leader. I am merely an individual who has set upon himself the task, if you will pardon the pun, of enforcing decency, integrity, and the respect for human lives in this terrible world of ours."

He walked up to the podium that until now had sat prominently but still unused at the front of the room and began to tell all present his ideas regarding the establishment of the Gatestrian Knights. He spoke of how the world fell to a battle of good versus evil, and how the rest of the planet failed to realize the tremendous responsibility that each individual had in regards to permitting or preventing what happened.

Jason spoke eloquently about their place in history, and how events of the past would've been averted had, for example, Europe forced Hitler out of power before he took over much of the continent. He continued with his ideas on how the present did not matter as importantly as did the future – the *far* future.

The implications of their actions was underscored and Jason repeatedly spoke of his views versus common good and requested the input from all; that no man's opinion would be sacrificed, that no man would be forced to conduct actions for which he did not believe to be ethical or even legal.

Finally, he apostrophized for the world's media. "Gentlemen, the good are often criticized because they are vulnerable, the bad often admired because they are unapproachable. We must accomplish our duties, not just because they are valid, but because they are needed. If we refuse to act because the world may consider us to be immoral, then we may have just earned that title anyway."

JASON STOOD SILENTLY on the tarmac, shielding his eyes with his right hand as he watched the lumbering C-130 cargo aircraft empty their bowels at the airport before heading back onto the runway and lifting off for points both secret and diverse.

He had been standing there for nearly an hour, watching the activities of no less than twenty aircraft, and was soon surrounded by droves of Land Rovers, Steyr 12 M 21 and Volvo 4140 trucks, as well as a host of other, larger military hardware that came up through Kenya bearing 'agricultural' supplies.

It had been two days since he ordered a massive buildup of forces, an activity forcibly objected to by President Baroque-Zambi until Jason had pledged nearly $1 Billion in economic aid over the course of the next ten years. He had now fully adopted Jack's infant nation, and set his sights upon the north.

Surrounded by such commotion and activity, Jason felt somewhat at ease; he had lost himself within the traffic and felt as if he was alone, and could concentrate on his thoughts. By nature, he never liked meetings or briefings, and would always find a way to excuse himself from them, preferring to remain within his own little world, and allowing his subordinates the luxury of planning free of his interference.

He did not possess any drastic mental abnormalities, perhaps no more than any other human being on the planet. What he did express, however, was the lack of desire for human companionship, at least from any individual other than his wife. He knew that he had changed, and changed drastically since her death.

His belief in religion, for instance, was placed to the test. He believed that this was entirely normal, given the circumstances, but somehow felt that he questioned God's influence upon the world a bit more than he had in the past. Not direct questioning, rather an incredulous frustration that the Lord remained fairly distant when things were going against common sense, a feeling that God no longer, or never did, take an active role in altering human history.

Jason always prayed, always attended church. Now, however, he felt that all was not well with the expectations that he had taken for granted in decades past. Samantha's death had hit home the prospect that maybe, just maybe, God required a very high price for entrance into Heaven.

This was the thought that he carried in his mind as he watched the military vehicles bring in weapons, ammunition, and medical supplies by the ton. Items that served no purpose but to inflict injury and death upon fellow human beings.

On occasion, Jason had the clarity of conscience to question as to what authority he had to judge who was evil and who was good. Yet, he could not forget the images of those butchered children and swore that he would, at a minimum, bring wrath against those who had committed such atrocities.

Jason Task had set himself up as judge, jury, and executioner of the villains of the world, a decision that required tremendous ego at best, and tremendous insanity at worst.

In a little over a week, he would decide whether to send troops north into Sudan in an attempt to remove that nation's military dictator. In spite of this critical decision, this entire operation had little to do with his overall plan. It merely reined as a convenient opportunity to test equipment and tactics, and to evaluate whether his new organization could do what Tactical Extractions had never been designed to do – wage long-term operations.

So Jason stood there, watching a massive military task force develop right before his eyes and realized that it was all a *private* effort and excluded any governmental participation whatsoever. Even the South Sudanese and the U.S. Central Intelligence Agency had no part of this operation. Should he give the go-ahead for the mission, he believed that he would initiate something probably unheard of in the annals of recent human history.

Nearly being run over by an exceptionally enthusiastic driver, Jason's train of thought was interrupted just long enough to notice an approaching individual.

"Mr. Task? My name is Chet Jennings."

"Oh yes, I wanted to talk to you." Jason reached over and shook the soldier's extended hand. "Because of your discovery, we may be going after the northern government."

"I'm ready." replied Jennings, eager to serve justice for the tragedy that he had discovered. "Just say the word."

A group of vehicles delayed Jason's reply, and he was eager to speak to the soldier for he wanted to temper his anger. "That's fine, but I would like for you to volunteer for another, no less important mission. I want for you to return to the States."

"The States?"

"Yes. I want you to take your story directly to the people and the media. I want you to let the entire country know what you found, how you found it, and why we must fight hard to stop these bastards from doing things like this in the future."

"Let me go back into action, sir, and I'll do just that."

Jason smiled. "That's good, but we've got a long mission to perform, and we won't be able to do it if the world jumps on the bandwagon against us. This is more than just revenge."

"Oh?"

"Yeah. Much, much, more."

Jason led Jennings over to a quieter part of the airport and explained to him his multi-year, indeed multi-decade plan for saving the world from villains such as the one who ordered the brutal murder of the innocent babies.

He went on to explain that the South Sudanese mission – now to include possibly operations against the northern Republic of Sudan as well – was nothing but a minor part of a truly global mission. The fact that Jason's plans ultimately included moving humanity off of the planet didn't seem to sway the attention of his soldier, but he abruptly stopped the narrative there just to be safe.

"The point is." concluded Jason. "We need to get popular opinion on our side early on."

"I'm yours to command." replied Jennings.

"Thank you."

While Chet Jennings departed to return back to his base at the forward operational area, Jason began a slow stroll back towards the command center, followed closely by his security personnel who were always near enough to respond to any crisis yet far enough away to avoid interrupting his daily life.

The only location where his security team didn't intrude was on the Jagged T, and Jason began to wonder whether he'd ever get to see the ranch again. With each passing vehicle, he knew that he wasn't simply gearing up for battle, he was gearing up for global conquest.

The battle against evil would take on epic proportions, or it would be his swan song, landing him squarely in a grave.

11

THE GROUP OF mottled-gray C-130s roared off the end of the runway, their four Rolls-Royce AE2100D3 turboprop engines charged quickly with the task of gaining speed, indifferent to the normal requirement of altitude.

Today's mission was neither routine nor training in nature, and the six blades of each Dowty Aerospace R391 propeller churned not for the nominal operating altitude of eighty-five hundred meters, but for the dangerously low sum of less than one hundred.

The four aircraft of Group Nine Seven banked steeply towards the northeast, hugging the White Nile to the left and making a beeline for Khartoum and the newly constructed Presidential Palace located deep within the heart of the ancient city.

The rate of travel and low altitude didn't leave much room for error as the pilots of the lead aircraft gazed out through the windscreens, calling out obstacles and landmarks with seemingly incoherent rapidity. The troops stationed within the cargo hold of the aircraft hung on for dear life as the plane buffeted and banked, turning first one way then another and finally back again.

The twenty members of the assault team were exercising various methods of dealing with the two hour, hair-raising flight. Some remained quiet, contemplating their assignments for when they stormed the heavily fortified palace. Some chewed gum quickly, trying to keep their minds – and their stomachs – off of the repeated bouncing that they had long since sacrificed their spines to suffer through. Others simply spoke quietly amongst themselves, preferring to chalk up the mission as just another escapade in their long resume of covert operations.

Group Nine Seven's aircraft flew in an extremely tight diamond formation, more so than any of the pilots would've cared for, considering that the entire mission was designed and trained for in less than a week. Its purpose being the lightning quick removal of a hostile dictator in support of a ground assault that would commence as soon as the target was secured.

The commandos were armed with a mix of silenced H&K MP5 and Uzi submachine guns, as well as M-16A4 rifles and an assortment of pistols. However, most important within their arsenal was the electro-dynamic stun grenade, a device that could flash a 100,000 volt plasma and effectively drop anyone within a three meter radius. The EDS grenade was extremely valuable in subduing hostiles without the need for deadly force.

The mission for which the group of aircraft sped towards could not have been attempted had it not been for timely intelligence that General Kuraymahiyyun was entertaining a late night guest in the form of Ms. Rosaria Pierre, the international opera star, following the 11:00 P.M. curfew imposed upon the city for all non-military activities. If all things went well, the General and his guest would be within the palace and more than likely finishing the evening with a nightcap when Group Nine Seven arrived at midnight.

Unfortunately the city of Khartoum resided approximately four hundred kilometers north of South Sudan's Upper Nile province, which meant at least forty-five minutes of the flight would be over hostile terrain with the prospect of detection looming over the entire operation.

What they had going for them, however, was the element of surprise. Even with the ground buildup south of the border, Kuraymahiyyun showed no signs of concern that the forces in the south would act against his overwhelming forces, a strong prediction based soundly on established historical precedence.

History, of course, had not had enough time to become acquainted with the likes of Jason Task and his policy of making seemingly irrational decisions in the name of progress. Group Nine Seven epitomized this new line of thought, and at the moment, raced towards implementation of its benefits.

One hour and forty-five minutes into the flight, the aircraft lined up with the northward turn of the White Nile and the troops that prepared to exit the low flying aircraft were warned of their impending departure.

"Fifteen minutes!" called out Jefferson Winkley, a towering figure who was at ease with his MP5 as much as he was with a Fender Stratocaster in his garage-style Winkley Rhythm & Blues Band. He reached over with his left foot and kicked a snoozing soldier. "Wake up Bartlett! They haven't killed us yet!"

The now awake but still groggy Gavin Bartlett stood up, merely reaching the chest of his much more massive commander. "Where are we?"

"Flying into hell's kitchen!" retorted Winkley as he walked along the line of commandos, rousing everyone up with his commands. "Stand up you sorry assed losers! Hook up! Jamison don't forget your medical bag! Thomason don't forget your parachute!"

Standing up within the highly buffeting aircraft was difficult, but finally all twenty men were in position. A group of five would each exit out through the side doors, and the remaining ten would egress through the aircraft's now opening cargo ramp, the lights of urban development rapidly flowing past the aircraft's belly and began to filter into the otherwise dark cabin interior.

A silhouette from the front of the cabin held up his palm with the barely visible fingers separated. "Five minutes!"

"Okay! Showtime you pansies!" roared Winkley as he focused his eyes on the jump light, knowing full well that his team – indeed all four teams – had mere seconds in which to exit their aircraft.

As the racing aircraft approached the drop zone nestled within the city that occupied the western bank of the Blue Nile, the tremendous buffeting ceased, a not quite comforting indication that it had zeroed in on its target and that it and all those who were within it no longer had the advantage of defensive maneuvering. It had to fly the straight and narrow in order that the troops could bail out without excessive danger.

Still, everyone aboard knew that many dangers existed, the primary one being the jumping out of an aircraft traveling at nearly a hundred and seventy five knots barely above the rooftops of the concrete structures that blazed by below.

Winkley watched as the red light flashed first to yellow then seconds later to green. "Go!" he screamed as he led the majority of the team out through the rear cargo opening.

Within a matter of seconds, the four aircraft disgorged a cloud of billowing olive drab parachutes barely visible against the black pearl night and vanished into the north amidst a dying rumble that faded after a few more seconds.

The parachutes, widely scattered as they were, remained aloft for a very short period of time before their operators descended upon selected target areas around the perimeter of the compound and, without prompting, headed off to conduct their particular mission.

The palace itself was a solidly built structure of white marble and red granite, consisting more of several smaller structures linked together via roofed corridors than a solitary complex, its artistic heritage from ancient Greek and Egyptian architecture being readily apparent.

General Kuraymahiyyun had wasted no time in creating the extravagant presidential residence once his forces had overthrown the previous government, his exceptional ego demanding a palace that far exceeded anything within the region.

Although not quite a year old and nowhere near completed, the sprawling facility was no match for the eighty well-armed and trained commandos that appeared seemingly out of nowhere and scattered among its ornate columns and buttresses.

MALCOLM WHITTAKER-KINCAID virtually gnawed a piece of his pipe off as he marched down the line of MCV-80 Warrior Infantry Fighting Vehicles and the dune buggy inspired U.S. Fast Attack Vehicles as he tugged repeatedly at his thick, graying handlebar mustache, barking out orders that kept his men in line.

"People this is not damn Boot Camp!" he bellowed out. "You are professionals now!"

The line of vehicles stood at the ready, their engines revving in preparation for the race across the border, the sound being the only thing that betrayed their existence to those who might be waiting concealed in darkness on the other side.

With the well-sculptured physique of a prize fighter and the ill-mannered patience of a bouncer, Whittaker-Kincaid shone his flashlight on his wristwatch, the red light illuminating the fact that it was precisely 12:00 A.M. "Move out!"

Within seconds, the massive ground force came to life and started to lead a trail of dust across the border into Sudanese territory. The MCV-80 Warriors scanning the horizon with night-vision capable RARDEN 30mm cannon and the FAVs scouting out the flanks with 7.62mm chain guns, .50-cal machineguns, and TOW anti-tank missiles.

Bringing up the rear were Spanish built Pegaso 3055 heavy trucks, each carrying thirty soldiers, interspersed with Brazilian ENGESA EE-9 Cascavel combat vehicles armed with 90mm guns as their primary weapon. Overhead, Sikorsky S-92 and S-76 helicopters roared on their way to support and retrieve the teams pouncing on the presidential residence.

This eastern group, combined with the western ground force which had its origins at Paradise Field, made up the brunt of the invasion of Sudanese territory. However, more covert operations had been initiated within the country's northwestern provinces where descendents of the Nubians felt betrayed by most ethnic Sudanese administrations, and most viciously persecuted by the current Kuraymahiyyun power circle.

Meeting minimal resistance, the eastern group raced up the road towards the towns of Al Jabalayn and Ad Duwaym and, ultimately, the capital, at a rate that would still take eleven hours to reach their destination if left uncontested.

Because the sole function of the foot soldier is simply to have someone occupy a plot of real estate, the two forces running towards Khartoum were intended to be merely that. The distances involved precluded any significant strategic advantage, particularly within a country of some 20 million inhabitants.

However, there was a singularly strategic advantage to having just such a small force unleashed upon an unsuspecting country – it created a diversion. The three-pronged attack of an invasion from the south, an insurrection in the northwest, and the raid on the capital could overwhelm an unprepared adversary just long enough to swing the odds and, perhaps, carry out the objectives set forth.

Unlike most military conflicts, this particular one had no expectations of conquering real estate – Jason Task had made certain of this – its sole purpose was to remove a hostile dictator from power who would have prevented more important missions from unfolding.

Malcolm Whittaker-Kincaid had been briefed on this very fact, and it was steadfast in his mind as he sat in the lead vehicle racing through the Sudanese night. He knew that, while they weren't exactly pawns, they weren't attacking a primary target either.

The Republic of Sudan, with or without General Kuraymahiyyun in charge, held no strategic purpose. It was not a *direct* threat. Most of all, even though Sudan contained vast reserves of important natural resources such as petroleum and natural gas, gold, manganese, zinc, iron, lead, uranium, copper, cobalt, nickel, and tin, to name but a few, they weren't readily available and significant investments were required to extract these resources.

In spite of this, Whittaker-Kincaid knew that Sudan had been a trouble spot for years, and a secret training base for Iranian terrorists since at least 1992. Added to their own nuclear ambitions, elements such as uranium and cobalt could prove disastrous, either as a cobalt laced nuclear or radiological bomb, potentially killing hundreds of thousands if allowed into the wrong hands.

Therefore, the muscular Brit knew that this was more than likely the reason for the recently hatched plot to remove Kuraymahiyyun from power and accordingly, he committed his efforts to this task wholeheartedly.

The race up to Khartoum, however, was largely uneventful with only a smattering of nocturnal creatures that temporarily slowed the progress. Human contact was concentrated near the towns of Al

Jabalayn and Ad Duwaym, where the locals surprisingly paid little heed to the convoy, perhaps believing that the troops were Sudanese on patrol or in training.

Whittaker-Kincaid stressed the importance of stealth and, failing that, obscurity. Movement was made without lights, communications, or erratic behavior. In short, the group raced towards the capital as if it was fairly routine to have over a hundred vehicles flying down the road in the middle of the night.

Such surprise, however, was misleading and he knew it. The reason, he concluded, that they met with zero resistance was undoubtedly because the one individual who would've issued orders to repel all attackers at all costs was, at the moment, fighting for his own life. In this regard, the military forces of which he served had achieved the ultimate in tactical warfare – they reached their objective before anyone knew they were coming.

JASON TASK PACED nervously in front of the projection screens that adorned the walls of the Communications Center at Paradise Field, first examining the one that projected images from the cameras carried by Group Nine Seven, then he turned his attention to the large map that displayed the progress of the units coming up from the south. Occasionally, he would permit a cursory glance at one of the other screens that showed the whereabouts of all aircraft, the position of the teams aiding the descendants of the Nubians in the northwest, or the monitor that ran material lists and usage reports.

The information that appeared on the screens within the large room, which was bathed within a dark blue light from the covered fluorescent lamps, changed quickly and it was difficult for him to keep tabs on all of the activities. Fortunately, the only real trouble appeared to be that coming from the Presidential Palace where enemy tracer fire could be seen coming from the hostile forces guarding the complex.

By all accounts, the raid had been moving swiftly and productively, with minimal friendly casualties and extensive hostile casualties. Jason was pleased with the way everything had been transpiring, based upon the limited knowledge that he had access to.

The absence of any coded messages that would indicate major failures or surprises also indicated that all was going smoothly.

He turned his attention to the images beaming in from Khartoum where the activities seemed to be winding down, a fact inspired by the appearance of two of his soldiers standing around what appeared to be a couple of incapacitated bodies with their hands folded. Nearby, another soldier stood guard with his MP5 at the ready.

Jason looked at the aircraft locations screen and saw several red dots moving towards the capital flanked by other yellow dots.

"What are those?" he asked, pointing towards the large screen.

"Our helicopters." replied Christopher Kent, Jason's aide. "Red indicates S-92s and the yellow ones are S-76s; Troopships and gun ships, respectively."

"How long before they reach the palace?"

"Oh, I'd say twenty minutes or so. We're not taking much interference."

Jason wrung the frustration out of his hands. "I suspect that will change as soon as it's daylight and the world media organizations get wind of what's going on. If they haven't already."

Chris Kent nodded in agreement, then added "If we're lucky, we might be in control of the country by daybreak."

"I wish."

As much as Jason would've liked that scenario, he knew that as soon as word got out as to what had happened, the shit would hit the fan. This meant that his organization would be labeled as simple mercenaries and the government of President Baroque-Zambi of the south would be targeted for oppositional harassment. He knew that both of their careers – and ultimately lives – depended upon how much he could persuade the court of world opinion that General Kuraymahiyyun was an evil figure who simply had to go.

Jason also knew a very important fact; A dead general meant a possible martyr, and the press just loved to attribute heroic deeds to dead assholes. Because of this reality, Group Nine Seven had been instructed to capture the general *alive,* along with as many of his henchmen as possible.

"Any word yet on the Butcher?" questioned Jason.

"Negative." replied one of the many computer operators who sat intently at their controls, giving Jason the impression that he was back at one of his spacecraft control centers, and why not, for all that he knew his organizations kept the same suppliers.

"When will we know anything?"

"I cannot answer that at the moment Mr. Task, but all indications are that there was a lot of EDS grenades going off. Perhaps they nabbed a target or two."

"I sure as hell hope so."

Jason crossed his fingers, knowing that the entire operation rested upon a basic fundamental fact that humans, as with all other animals of nature, had a built-in trait that prevented the destruction of like species.

Translated into military advantage, this trait ensured that most people would either elect to fire above the heads of other people or otherwise attempt to fake their actions. This response fell under the psychological term of *posturing* – one of only four possible reactions to combat and, broadly defined, showed that humans, much like any other animal, tried to inflate their stature in an attempt to induce flight or submission into their foe.

Elk, for example, would gladly gore an attacking wolf to death, but when another elk threatened their prominence, they simply locked horns and wrestled until either capitulated and simply retreated into the woods. It was a simple fact that permitted the continuation of a species.

Posturing was widely evident within military history. Napoleonic-era soldiers wore extravagant hats that served no practical function other than to inflate their size and Confederate soldiers of the American Civil War had their rebel yell which not only scared the hell out of some Union soldiers but also motivated the charging troops in order to attack vastly superior numbers.

Posturing, Jason knew, also had a detrimental effect, such as when it was discovered that eighty-five percent of U.S. soldiers in World War II didn't fire their rifles at the enemy or during Vietnam when a Congressional report concluded that it averaged some 50,000 rounds to inflict a single casualty.

Throughout history, armies were more than likely to fire their weapons above the heads of the enemy, or even *continue* to load their weapons without having fired them in an effort to appear to be conducting battle while still managing to avoid firing at fellow human beings. In fact, most wartime casualties came from artillery or aircraft bombardment.

People could be classed into four categories. The first group consisted of average people who went about daily life without making virtually any decisions at all, much less those regarding the techniques required to kill a fellow citizen. The second group consisted of the protectors – the police and soldiers of the world – those citizens who seemed to belong to the first group owing to their decency and loyalty, but who would stand tall and heroically defend the defenseless, even at the risk of their own lives.

The third group consisted of the villains, whose primary interest was the unabated destruction of lives and property in wolf-like fashion. The fourth group represented an evolution of the third, where many individuals combined to form gangs or terrorist organizations along the simple premise that more meant better.

Jason knew that people *did* in fact kill regardless of a subconscious disposition against doing so. They learned to kill by increasing the distances involved through the use of long-range artillery, aircraft, missiles, sniper rifles, and time bombs. If one couldn't *see* death, then one wouldn't be adverse to causing it.

This also explained why executions, both legal and illegitimate, were carried out with a bag over the person or a bullet through the *back* of their head – it removed the need for the executioner to look into the eyes of another human being while they promptly blew them away.

Dehumanization of the subject also increased the likelihood of someone being able to kill. If they were of a different skin color, or of a different faith, or of a different nationality, then somehow they became *less human* and therefore easier to kill.

Regardless, people of all persuasions shared a common tenet: they could only fight if they saw the enemy and *had time to react* to the situation. This fact led to centuries of attrition warfare, where opposing lines squared off neatly against each other and literally spent weeks, months, and even years hammering away at one another until either side gave way and fled, enabling the victor an opportunity to give chase and thereby returning to the concept of not looking your opponent in the eyes while he annihilated them.

Fear manifested itself in many ways within battle and the most prominent of these was having an enemy appear suddenly within *your backyard*. To face an intruder who was intent on violating your integrity within your own home territory was no less of a fear than a woman felt when she contemplates rape or when a homeowner realizes that they've been burglarized.

Forces suddenly finding themselves exposed to hostile attack behind friendly lines either capitulated rapidly or fled from the desire to stand firm and repel, the decision usually being sacrificed during the initial moments of confusion when the defenders cannot group, call for reinforcements or conjure up the motivation necessary to defend their homeland.

This was the basic knowledge that convinced Jason Task to launch a direct assault against General Kuraymahiyyun's palace, bypassing literally hundreds of thousands of Sudanese citizens who might've been persuaded or forced to defend their country.

By unleashing a lightning quick raid against unsuspecting forces, Jason's men could do what bureaucratic governments never had the inclination to do – end a conflict before it even had a chance to begin, thereby eliminating casualties and damage to the local infrastructure.

JEFFERSON WINKLEY ENTERED the main hall quickly, his MP5 at the ready, examining the surrounding environment with the inquisitive eyes of a seasoned artist. The two individuals on the floor were motionless, but still appeared alive. A man and a beautiful woman.

He saw several other bodies that laid strewn about the floor, bodies that were obviously just that, bodies without the human spirit animating them. Bodies that were tattered by 9mm bullets and a few whose throats were slit at the beginning of the assault. He counted seven that were shot to death and four that were silenced by way of Ka-Bar knives.

He had been drawn into the hall from the outer parapet by the noise of two EDS grenades and the resulting bluish flash of the electrically charged plasma that apparently incapacitated the two individuals.

"Is that the General?" He asked, staring at the individual whose face bore the contortions of being paralyzed by thousands of volts.

"I sure as hell hope so!" replied Gavin Bartlett, still somewhat shaken by the quick capture of the palace. "I don't think that our luck will hold out if we have to search the place again."

"Yeah. Then, I assume that's Ms. Pierre?"

"Fuck if I know." shrugged Bartlett. "Bitch tried to scratch me with her nails so I belted her."

"You didn't neutralize her with an EDS?"

"Hell no. I had to use *both* on the general. Bastard wasn't going down on one, so I shoved one down his shirt and let it off."

"Ouch!"

"Well, that's when Miss Opera Whore here came flying across the room screaming and hollering like she was a banshee or something. I grabbed her by the shoulder so she wouldn't warn the rest of the place and that's when she started swingin' those damn blades of hers and I belted the bitch just as hard as I could!"

Peter Jamison, one of the group's members who was also trained as a medic, trotted in from the north side of the compound. "Is that who I think it is?"

"Yeah." replied Winkley, kneeling down alongside his new arrival. "They *are* alive, aren't they?"

Jamison quickly set about examining the two individuals. "So far. The general has one hell of a burn across his chest. The woman is fine, but it looks like she has a broken jaw. What hit her?"

"I did." grumbled Bartlett who had diverted his attention from the subject by instinctively tying up the general's legs. "Dumb bitch tried to skewer me with those machetes of hers."

Jamison slowly shook his head in comedic disbelief. "Well, she'll live, but I'm still worried about this guy."

Winkley looked at his watch. "The choppers should be coming in soon. We can take him out. Thomason, where the hell are you?"

Warren Thomason came running into the main hall from an outer pathway. "The rest of the team has the perimeter surrounded. Slight casualties. Nothing major. We've got a shit load of prisoners to watch and the town is beginning to wake up and notice that something ain't exactly kosher around here."

"Well, they can have their town." snorted Winkley as he stood up. "We've come to take out the general and by God we did. Now, let's get the hell out of here and let the boss worry about how to handle the country." He looked again at the palatial residence. "Let's leave a calling card. Prepare to blow the place!"

"Right!" acknowledged Thomason as he quickly departed to retrieve a few cases of high explosives.

Jamison stood up, peeling the latex gloves from his hands. "We really need to get him out of here if he's to have any chance of surviving."

"He's that bad?"

"Well I don't think that it's necessarily the shock. He's got puncture wounds all over and I suspect that he's been using some narcotics."

"That explains why I had to use two grenades." added Bartlett shaking his head. "He just kept fighting and fighting and....hell, I bet the bitch is on drugs too!"

"Probably." offered Winkley. "Where the hell are those choppers?"

"Two minutes!" replied a voice from outside the main hall, its sound reverberating within the stone and marble building.

Off in the distance, the approaching helicopters made a direct run for the Presidential Palace, flying just a few meters above the waters of the White Nile heading towards its junction with the Blue Nile and Khartoum.

Sikorsky S-76s floated in a lazy circle pattern providing perimeter defense while the larger S-92s were to serve as the extraction platform for the prisoners whose rank warranted an immediate response, namely General Kuraymahiyyun and a few of his top aides.

Without restraint, the helicopter fleet soared up along the river, narrowly missing a small vessel and into the city whose easternmost boundary rested on the banks of the Blue Nile and turned inland and made their final dash towards the palace that had now become surrounded by some eighty well-trained and motivated visitors from the south.

The troop helicopters parked in a holding pattern because the main courtyard was only sufficiently large enough for one of them to land – rather hover a few meters off of the ground – at a time while the gun ships patrolled at varying degrees of distance.

The arrival of the aircraft initiated a response that, in ways, was considerably more vigorous than when the assault team had first descended upon the palace, but the difference being that the helicopter fleet was *expected*.

The sleepy residents of Khartoum still had no idea that their future had been altered, that their nation was now back into their hands, and that The Butcher who had unleashed his brief but severe rein of terror was now busily being hauled into one of the noisy helicopters that assailed their city during this otherwise most uneventful of nights.

Many of the residents who had the fortunate chance to have been awake or had been awaken by the commotion that erupted around the palace watched the first helicopter depart with haste, oblivious to the fact that the madman who had been but a brief footnote in their nation's long and colorful history was being hauled off to face justice and that their country of Sudan had the opportunity if not the motivation to establish a true democracy.

12

GROUND OPERATIONS COMMANDER Malcolm Whittaker-Kincaid leapt out of his vehicle, paused for a moment as he surveyed his surroundings, then began to jog up the red granite steps that led into the palace complex. He was a little apprehensive about the crowds that surrounded the presidential residence, and concluded that things might get out of hand once the locals realized what had happened during the night. He was more than a little surprised that they didn't already know that it wasn't Sudanese soldiers that had pulled into the heart of Khartoum in the middle of the day but had since realized that General Kuraymahiyyun had been known to employ foreign mercenaries, even white ones, so perhaps all wasn't as unusual as it first appeared.

He walked through the corridor that opened between the towering white columns, eyed several Sudanese and Arabic prisoners that were lined up against a far wall, then proceeded into the General's office which sat adjacent to the rear entrance. He was searching for a secluded place, or rather a partially secluded place, where he could write a preliminary report concerning the run up from the south.

In particular, he wanted to commit to paper the events that unfolded near the town of Ad Duwaym where they encountered their first, indeed only, resistance and engaged in a brief firefight that resulted in one hundred hostile casualties and ten friendly casualties. This action delayed their arrival into Khartoum until 2:00 P.M. and by then the mission at the palace had already been long completed and the crowds gathered.

Near Ad Duwaym, they had destroyed several Sudanese tanks which alerted the locals as to their presence and brought in reinforcements. However, Whittaker-Kincaid wisely elected not to oblige them in combat and directed his victorious troops to continue on to Khartoum.

He was now wondering whether these additional troops were also on their way to the capital to force his hand. With General Kuraymahiyyun gone, they were now in harm's way with no purpose but to secure the site and, hopefully, make an exit towards the south. If the reinforcements from Ad Duwaym were on their way up, then he'd have to fight his way through them.

His planning was hamstrung by one of several factors. First, the Sudanese strongman was out of the country and in their hands. This meant that *someone* had to take his place, possibly from the general's own people. This successor could be more favorable than the general himself or he could be far worse, opening a whole new can of worms.

The second problem concerned the Sudanese people themselves. For good or bad, his forces removed the lid on a boiling pot with no resources available to contain the overflow. Where they excelled over Western nations in military effectiveness, they were handicapped by not having an effective political arm that could move in and contain the problems left open by the overthrow of a despot.

At best, this meant rioting in the streets. At worst, it meant another long-term civil war. The first option would be like a tornado which is powerful and deadly, but relatively short in duration. Peaceful forces could quickly put down such chaos and restore order within a few days at most. The prospects of a civil war would be slow in coming, much like a hurricane, but it would leave much more damage behind that would take longer – significantly longer – to clean up after.

For the moment, Whittaker-Kincaid worried about getting his men out of harm's way. He had considered using Khartoum's airport as an extraction point, but that entailed leaving hundreds of vehicles, weapons, and ammunition behind. This would be akin to praying for either a tornado or hurricane.

He decided that his best chance was to create the impression that his forces were stronger than they actually were. Along with this, he had to reduce the fighting capability of the existing Sudanese forces without actually destroying their ability to fight and, accordingly, contain local uprisings.

Because ninety percent of the Sudanese forces were either ill-trained conscripts or soldiers who were forced to swear allegiance to Kuraymahiyyun, he decided that the best option was to reduce the level at which the Sudanese forces were allowed to congregate. He knew that unit cohesion was a fundamental part of battle efficiency; few wanted to be known as the weak link in any chain and the fear that a unit may be destroyed because of one's failure to perform was in itself a powerful motivating factor.

Analyzing his options, Whittaker-Kincaid elected to utilize the Khartoum airport in a reverse method. He decided to call in reinforcements which could land in the capital and shore up his forces. Then, the whole group would make their way south, probably along secondary roads leading towards the southwest – towards Paradise Field – where they could meet up with the Western Ground Forces Group and then turn south.

By taking advantage of this redirection and group rendezvous, he could be assured of defeating any forces that the Sudanese could muster. All of this, of course, depended on what The Boss wanted to accomplish.

JASON TASK SAT on the large red sofa with his feet laid out along its length, a stack of post-action reports straddling his lap. He was deeply impressed with the quick and efficient capture of the general, a little apprehensive about the local population which seemed to be taking everything in stride, and very concerned over the hundreds of his men who were now sitting pretty much idle in hostile territory.

He knew that his good fortune was largely due to the shock imposed upon both the Sudanese military and its population, a stroke of luck he also knew would come crashing down as soon as everyone was able to step back and realize what had just happened. Then, he knew, the world's media organizations would come in by the hordes blasting him as a war monger, villain, anti-humanitarian, you name it, never minding that the general and his mistress were still alive, there was insignificant collateral damage, and relatively few hostiles killed.

Jason, at the moment, wanted most to get his men south of the border and position South Sudan in a defensive mode. This would permit him time to access the situation, and perhaps negotiate some economic package with whomever took control of the north.

He tapped his fingers in rhythmic fashion on the request that had come in a few minutes earlier from his on-site commander regarding additional forces to land at Khartoum's international airport. Jason liked the idea of withdrawing to the southwest and linking up with the western group, but wondered whether this would place his men in jeopardy by exposing them to an extended journey.

Two things made his men succeed so far. First, they attacked the palace in a lightning quick raid *prior* to undertaking any other operation, thereby accomplishing their goal before they really had the chance to begin. Second, the ground forces exercised maneuver warfare and raced directly towards the capital without stopping to engage most of the hostile forces that they came into contact with.

Now, things were different. A retreat towards the southwest could not be conducted as quickly as the northward run had been for the roads were relatively minor and rarely used. More importantly, however, his men were now known to be within the capital and the Sudanese Army, or at least what was left of it, would be hunting for them.

Jason was smart enough to know that he wasn't a military commander which is why he spent millions hiring those who were. He had trusted Whittaker-Kincaid's decisions on the way up and he knew that he could trust his commander's judgment on getting his men out of Khartoum in a hurry. That wasn't the problem. What was, was getting him sufficient reinforcements to battle both hostile forces and a pissed off public on the way out.

"Mr. Kent." called Jason to his aide who occupied a desk at the far end of the office. "How can we act on this request?"

"Well, Mr. Task." Chris Kent had been intently studying the facts and figures of the operation, trying to determine their material strengths and weaknesses, as well as their manpower capabilities. After a few seconds, he looked up from his papers. "We're a little short on ground forces, but we can airlift some men into the capital."

Jason said nothing, but considered the irony. Here was a man who made a sizeable portion of his fortune by assisting people in getting out of the world's trouble spots and now he wasn't sure if he could *get his own men out of trouble.* "C'mon, Jace. Think!"

"Excuse me, sir?"

"Just thinking aloud."

"A problem?"

"Nothing that *we* of all people shouldn't be able to handle."

"Certainly."

"First, let's find some more equipment and find it fast. On the subject, we need to start acquiring more modern equipment; our forces went into battle with vehicles that were nearly ten to fifteen years old in some cases."

"Our choppers are new."

"Yes, but damn expensive. If we're going to remain an effective military force and not just a snatch and grab operation, we need to have modern equipment and advanced technology."

Kent nodded briefly, then returned to his paperwork.

Jason glanced at his Rolex. It was 4:05 P.M. In an hour he would be sitting in on an interrogation of General Kuraymahiyyun, his last scheduled event before he departed Africa for the United States and, in his opinion, sanity. Responsibility for Sudanese operations would ultimately be turned back over to Jack Stephens so that Jason could concentrate on building the Gatestrian Knights into a solid organization.

He wanted to get back home, but knew there would be hell to pay for his role in the overthrow of the existing, if not legitimate, Sudanese government. For all that he knew, he would be placed in handcuffs as soon as he landed and hauled off to some dingy federal prison.

To avoid this very real possibility, he had three things going for him – a wealth of historical precedence that fell squarely on his side, namely the Flying Tigers of World War II fame and the verdict of the late Robert F. Kennedy offering that such activities by Americans were not necessarily illegal; his decision to pad the campaign budgets of several prominent politicians on both sides of the aisle; and the decision that he was going to send his executive jet back empty as a ruse while he entered the United States under clandestine measures.

Then, of course, there were his many missions conducted through the auspices of Tactical Extractions which had both excelled in remaining unattached from him directly and the experience to deal with these sorts of legal issues over the course of the past decade. Jason didn't have a fifty thousand square foot building full of constitutional and international law attorneys for nothing.

Actually, all of this was fairly old hat for the man who continued to grow weary of established authority. He loved the United States, loved it dearly, but he also had a strong hatred of the politicians who wanted to rein in its greatness for the sake of international relations, particularly with Europe which Jason despised with a passion.

For now, however, he had to forget about the United States, Europe, even himself. He had to bring his men back quickly and safely, and where his men were concerned, he spared nothing.

THE CROWDS THAT had surrounded the palace buzzed with mixed levels of excitement, some being concerned about the presence of the newcomers, while others complained about the snarl in the evening traffic. Rumors had been spread that General Kuraymahiyyun was enforcing his grip upon the Sudanese nation, but most insiders knew that the soldiers present didn't wear Sudanese uniforms.

The desert camos and purple berets were different, and not recognized among even the rabble who could barely be expected to know who was in power and for how long. The street merchants and businessmen, however, had a strange feeling that something was amiss, but in Khartoum these days, no one could be certain of anything.

Even the handcuffed Sudanese soldiers who were led to the waiting Land Rovers didn't raise an alarm, with most residents assuming that they were disloyal to the General or otherwise had broken one of his many laws.

Slowly, however, word came flowing in from the southern provinces that an invasion of their sovereign nation by South Sudan had been carried out. The locals weren't exactly sure if they, the city itself, had been the victim of enemy action, and the confusion remained partly because no one really wanted to know whose side the well-armed, purple bereted soldiers were on.

Malcolm Whittaker-Kincaid was equally concerned and figured that his men had only an hour or two left before all hell broke loose within the capital. His brisk walk throughout the complex to ensure that explosive charges had been set did nothing to ease his mind. Soon, the whole damn place could be covered with innocent people and he wanted to bug out before anything went wrong.

He hoped – prayed, that the commercially marked C-130s that began arriving at the airport bearing food and medical supplies would create a diversion long enough for his men to make a run for the southwestern border. The planes, bearing the name of the non-profit McIntyre Foundation, would bring hope to a nation ravaged by decades of civil war and famine, as well as city that sat atop a virtual time bomb of transitory politics.

It had been about eighteen hours since Sudan's future was altered, only a brief span of time within the ancient country that changed leaders with the weather. The haze from the city's business district hug softly in the air as normal, indicating that commercial activity had not been sidelined by the events that transpired at the stroke of the day.

Whittaker-Kincaid pulled a tobacco pouch out of his left chest pocket, unraveled it, and poured some of its contents into his smoldering pipe, taking a few brief puffs to stoke the embers. The aroma of tobacco reminded him of his childhood, his father, and of times far removed from the present.

Gordon Tyler, the team's demolitions expert, was busy stringing the final lines of detonating cord through the main hall. "The charge's are set, sir. We'll be ready when you are."

"Fine." Malcolm removed his pipe momentarily, releasing a puff of bluish-white smoke that seemed to float throughout the entire complex, buoyed by the stale, humid air. "We'll be pulling out shortly."

While Tyler ran the final lines out through the front doors and into the streets, Whittaker-Kincaid continued to make his rounds, ordering all personal out of the complex, and dispatching a select team to enforce crowd control.

When the explosives went off, he knew, the whole city would be informed that things were now totally different.

Paul Santini, a tall, muscular individual whose past life included posing for the covers of romantic novels entered the main hall, hurriedly searching for Malcolm. "The crowd's beginning to realize that things aren't what they appear." Nervousness had his voice one octave higher than normal. "Even the beggars know primacord when they see it."

The Ground Forces Commander nodded, slowly tapping the end of his pipe against his chin, mentally going through the final check list before he gave the orders to evacuate the facility. After several more minutes, the pipe found its mark and he drew in one, final breath before dumping the burning tobacco onto the floor. "Let's do it."

"Right." Santini moved swiftly into the front street, his M-16A4 motioning the crowds to head back towards the far side of the street. Some didn't obey, but once the locals saw that his rifle was leveled directly at them, they capitulated and quickly exited the area.

Whittaker-Kincaid was the last person to leave the building and walked authoritatively over to his Land Rover, surveying his team's handling of the crowds in the process.

"Five minutes!" he called out, not wishing to waste a single second.

His team knew that the warning was less of a command for safety than as an acknowledgement that as soon as the explosives were detonated, they would immediately be on the road heading to their escape route. Nobody wanted to hang around when the locals saw them destroy Khartoum's beloved, if somewhat infamous palace.

The burly commander took a final glimpse of the extravagant palace, fighting a feeling of remorse over its pending destruction. Having ventured all over the world, he'd become something of an armchair architect and wanted to preserve the structure. Still, he knew what the building represented, who was sacrificed for its construction, and what the message would be for the world's despots once it was reduced to rumble.

With a final scan of the surroundings, he gave a quick wave of his hand. "Do it!"

"Fire in the hole!" cried a voice that simultaneously seemed to come from everywhere, followed close behind by several muffled bangs, then several louder thuds.

The first indication that anything unusual was happening for the residents of the neighborhood was the outpouring of smoke and debris from the interior of the building that spiraled around some of the columns before rising up into the darkening sky.

Soon after, the inner most marble columns began to cascade inwards, followed in short order by the larger, more ornate structural columns of the outer perimeter. What moved in slow motion at first, quickly accelerated in pace until the only thing that could be rationalized by the human thought process was the downward collapse of the building's red granite roof.

The crowds who had encircled the facility had been pushed back by the sound of the explosions, only to return in force as if drawn in by the vacuum created from the palace's destruction. The quiet murmur that had been simmering all day erupted into various chants of anger, pleasure, frustration, and fear.

The troops who had destroyed the marvelous structure required no further instructions as what to do, and by the time the reverberations of the explosions fell silent, were well on their way through the busy streets of the city.

As planned beforehand, the exodus was carried out in three directions, splitting the force into what appeared to be a massive overtaking of the city, only to recombine near the southwest corridor and begin the long trek towards the waiting Western Group where both units could head directly south to Paradise Field.

GENERAL KURAYMAHIYYUN HAD sat bound to the chair, stripped to his shorts, for hours without saying anything or having anyone say a word to him. In fact, the dozens of people who walked into or through the room literally paid no attention to the individual who watched everything that went on.

On two separate occasions, Jason Task walked within inches of the general, paused as if to say something, then continued to undertake some innocent task as retrieve a stapler, or throw some papers into the trash. Nobody even seemed to care that the general was there, but they did.

Jason was more inclined to beat the shit out of the bastard, but he wanted facts. He wanted to have as many details regarding the torture and death of the innocent babies found by his men. Knowing that the general wouldn't be inclined to talk, and knowing that the world would detest any physical harm against the general, Jason elected to break down the captive's resolve through other means.

When confronting an individual with an ego as massive as was the general's, this was easy – you *ignored* them completely. The more the captive realized that they were being reduced to nothing, the more it inflamed their sense of pride and anger.

Emotion was a powerful motivator when it came to getting a tight-lipped individual to spill the beans, and it would be only a matter of time before an egocentric strongman like Kuraymahiyyun found the *need* to communicate with someone.

The general knew, had to know, that he was captured because of his deeds. He was whisked out of his palace under armed guard because he was the dangerous and powerful savior of the Sudanese people. His enemies were legion, and wanted solely to destroy his beloved nation and its faithful. *Why didn't anyone want to talk to him?*

Another two hours passed before Jason and Chris Kent walked into the room, talking about the latest football scores, before selecting chairs within arm's reach of the bound dictator. Shortly afterward, a third individual arrived, a pleasant looking individual dressed in a white cotton jacket and sporting a medium length ponytail and round, wire rimmed glasses. The newcomer, looking more like a throwback to the folk era of the sixties than a military person, preceded to park himself across a table from Jason and Chris.

"I would like to exercise my rights as a journalist." spoke the newcomer, taking a small notebook out of his jacket. "To interview the prisoner."

Jason's face turned somewhat flush, a burst of anger manifesting itself down along the curvature of his face, but he chose his words carefully. "I have already made my decision, Mr. Smith. There will be no interviews permitted with the general."

"May I remind you." retorted Wade Smith, not disguising any anger. "That I have the power to expose your organization's atrocities against this individual?"

"Atrocities?" Jason nearly choked, and had to retrieve a Diet Coke® from the nearby refrigerator to wash down the distaste within his mouth. "This bastard here was the one that committed the atrocities! Who's looking out for all of those mutilated babies?"

Wade Smith casually noticed the general's level of interest in the debate increase, indicating a certain knowledge of the English language, a fact reinforced by prior intelligence. His observation of the general matched certain key words and phrases that he had been looking for, and once he felt comfortable that the general was primed, signaled his thoughts to the others by placing his notepad down onto the table and folding his arms across his chest, feigning frustration.

On cue, Jason bitched about liberal journalists spouting laws and stressed the need for some fresh air, ordering Chris Kent to keep the visitor from talking to the prisoner while he stormed out of the room.

As planned well beforehand, exactly forty-five minutes after the departure of Jason, Kent quietly maneuvered himself out of the room under the premise of heading to the lavatory, leaving Wade Smith and General Kuraymahiyyun as the room's sole occupants.

A few minutes later, Smith glanced over and made direct eye contact with the general, the first such recognition of anybody that the general was even located within the room. This act did not go unnoticed by the bound prisoner.

Smith allowed a slight nod, then after a few more minutes, whispered "*Hal talkallam Ingliizi?*"

The general did not answer, but Smith could tell by the response of his eyes that the prisoner wanted to say yes, but chose to remain steadfast.

Smith redirected his approach. "*Turiid tashrab?*"

The general thought long and hard about accepting a drink, but still refrained from answering.

Wade Smith decided to sweeten the pot and pulled a pack of cigarettes out of his jacket pocket, placed one into his mouth and lit it. "*Bitriid sigaara?*"

The general desperately wanted a cigarette, but grew increasingly suspicious of the foreign journalist.

"*Kiif haalak ya sayyidati?*" asked Smith calmly, almost motherly in his respect.

The general nodded slowly, but remained silent, cautiously examining his surroundings, especially the side exits.

Smith suspected that the general was beginning to lean towards his confidence, but feared arrival of either Jason or Chris Kent. "*Hal tatakallam Ingliizi?*" he asked again, lighting a Camel and placing it into the general's mouth.

"Yes." The general's voice was low, barely registering as a whisper. "I speak English."

Smith smiled, knowing that he was gaining the general's trust. "I want to talk to you before the other's come back. I want to interview you for my newspaper. Do you understand?"

"Yes."

"How did these people take you?" The question was meant to instill more confidence.

"They invaded my nation's sovereignty." The answer was more political than coerced, and the general wanted the world to know of his plight.

Smith sensed that the general was beginning to open up. "They told me that you ordered the killings of children, but I know that it was merely your men."

The general was weary, and knew that he deserved to be treated as a head of state, not as a common criminal. "I am General Kuraymahiyyun, President of the Republic of Sudan."

"Yes, yes. I know. Before they come back! Who killed the children?"

"Nobody killed any children."

Wade Smith knew the general was lying, avoiding the truth as he became more confident. "Somebody did. I heard one of your men say that *you* did it, but I don't believe it. You're a general, you only give orders for others to carry out. Right?"

"I am General Kuraymahiyyun."

"You have many followers."

"I am the Great...."

"With many, many followers. What is the name of the traitor who tarnished your image?"

The general was resistive, but tired and his body sore from lack of movement. "There are *no* traitors, I have eliminated all of them."

"Somebody said that you killed the babies. You only give orders."

"Yes, I do."

"Who's the traitor?"

"I don't allow any traitors."

"Who's the traitor that carried out your orders. Quickly! Before the others come!"

"Colonel Abu Faiz..."

"The colonel is the traitor? The one who carried out your orders to kill the babies?"

"The colonel killed them."

"Then the colonel is the traitor."

"I have no traitors. I do not permit them. I killed them all."

Smith knew that he had the general lined up where he wanted him, but knew that it would take a few more hours to pressure him into talking fully. Walking over to a Coke® machine that sat near the door, he placed in a few coins and retrieved a cold can of soda, the sound of the falling can echoing throughout the room, before returning to his original seat.

Precisely two minutes after the can of soda hit the bottom of the machine, and roughly thirty seconds after the general had finished his smoke, Jason Task entered the room with Chris Kent, arguing over what to do with the general.

Jason paused briefly after entering the room, sniffed around, then looked at the cigarette butt that sat smoldering on the floor. "Whose is this?" He retrieved the cigarette butt and flashed a vicious look towards Smith. "Did you give the general a cigarette!"

"I haven't left this chair since you left." explained Smith, doing his best to show his anger with the line of questioning.

"Then where the hell did this butt come from?"

Smith, slowly held up his own lit cigarette, then motioned towards the trash can that sat in the corner near the general. "I missed the trash can and I just didn't bother getting up. What's the fuckin' deal?"

Jason threw the cigarette butt into the trash can then violently kicked it across the room, startling both Chris Kent and the general. "I don't want anyone near the general!" He walked over and opened the side door. "Security!"

Two rugged looking guards came into the room, their M-16's held at the waist and proceeded to flank the general.

Jason untied the general who spent several minutes working out the soreness in his limbs. "Take the general to his room. Let no one, and I mean no one talk to him!"

"Yes, sir!" replied the guards in unison, escorting the overtly tired and irritated general out of the room.

Shortly after the door was closed behind them, Jason turned to Smith. "Get anything out of him?"

"Not much, it's going to take some effort to build his confidence in me. He doesn't believe that any of his people could go against him, so I don't think that we'll be able to convince him that he has traitors, and I wouldn't recommend it. Traitors would be either dead or too scared to admit their disloyalty. He did, however, implicate Colonel Abu Faiz, but we already knew that going in."

Jason nodded, straddled a chair backwards and sat down, resting his chin on its back. "How much time are you going to need?"

"Probably a couple of weeks to get much of anything out of him. You are aware that we've *already* removed him from office, right? We don't need very much information."

"Listen, if the janitor at the opera house had anything to do with those murdered babies, I want to know about it. This has nothing to do with who's in power in Khartoum. They murdered those babies simply because they were *Christian* babies. I want to know who carried out the task, who ordered the task, who benefited from the task. Everyone! Then, I want to set about finding out how to change a world that allows such things to happen."

Wade Smith shrugged his shoulders. "In other words, you staged a one-of-a-kind lightning raid into Khartoum, removed a person from power, then left the country to its own devices because babies were murdered?"

"I have a soft spot for babies." snapped Jason as he leapt up from his chair. "I used to be one myself."

"Ah, ha."

"Listen, Sudan *is* of strategic importance, don't get me wrong. Right now, however, I'm interested in South Sudan. Raiding Khartoum was just my way of sending a wake-up call to the world. A chance to say, 'Hey, throw away morals, and you'll have to deal with me!' Hopefully, the world will also learn that our military forces are far superior than many powerful nations. The media will have a field day with this event and, in turn, I'm going to have a field day with them."

"So how far do you want me to go with the general?" questioned Smith.

"I'll give you three weeks to find out all that you can. I have to return to the States now; I'm leaving as soon as our troops pull back into South Sudanese territory. Nobody knows where the general is, at the moment, and I'll only be able to stall for a week or two before this thing gets blown completely out of proportion. That's when we'll have to turn him over to the Red Cross or Red Crescent or somebody."

"I'll do what I can, but it won't be easy. Sooner or later he'll know that I'm not a journalist, and then he'll pucker up tighter than my ass on a caffeine binge. What then?"

"We're not diplomats. We're not true military. We're our own law out here. Interrogate him as *you* see fit. As for me, I've got to get back to the States. We have bigger things to worry about than whether some two-bit thug gets treated well."

13

THE BURGUNDY CURTAINED Task Tower was one of Houston's most innovative and well-recognized office buildings, soaring 57 stories into the azure sky, creating a contrast of color not represented anywhere else in the world. So new was this facility, that only the top twelve floors were currently occupied by administrative and executive personnel, whereas the bottom five were strictly retail.

The elongated heptagonal shaped facility made exceptional use of the diffraction of the raising and setting sun, and quickly became something of a cult icon for New Agers who believed that hidden messages were contained within each spectral exhibition.

Not to be outdone by the day, the corners of the facility were accented by beautifully lit waterfalls, themselves flanked by brilliant neon lights of all color persuasions. Inside of each waterfall, rode a glass encased elevator which ran the length of the five floor retail substructure.

What greeted visitors when they entered Task Tower, however, was absolutely spectacular – they were surrounded by numerous saltwater aquariums that seemed to outflank their every move. In fact, visitors did not merely walk around the aquariums, they walked *through* them, every store wall being another facet of the tank system.

Contrary to published opinion, the half billion dollar Task Tower was not simply an exercise in extravagance, its form followed function. Deep within its bowels was one of the largest supercomputer centers in the United States, a hospital, and a satellite communications center.

Perhaps the only thing regarding the massive complex that seemed somewhat uncharacteristic of Jason Task, was that the large building was not a dedicated facility – anyone could lease space in it, and although office spaces were widely available within the city, its retail capabilities were locked-in well into the future, indicating an acceptance by the purchasing public if not the corporate elite.

The cavernous conference center on the fifty-sixth floor could easily seat one hundred people at its large oak table, and frequently did. Today, however, merely thirty people occupied one end of the heavy table, listening to Jason lecture in front of the large projection screens, detailing many geopolitical facts about the world, his operations, and their expectations for the future.

"Ladies and gentlemen." he spoke. "I give you our world. Hostile, segregated, mismanaged, but still *our* world... as we know it. Three weeks ago, I returned from Africa, where I witnessed what man can do when pure evil inherits his heart. Yet, it was when I returned to the *civilized* world that I saw what evil manifested within man is really capable of doing."

Jason stepped to the side, so that his visitor's could view the large screen that carried the *Fox News Channel*, and hear a little of the conversation that it presented. Two men had been talking to the anchor regarding the exploits of Jason in Africa. One held the opinion that the operation was justified, the other that it broke all bounds of international law and that Jason Task should be charged with murder."

"My God, people." Jason continued, stepping in front of the screen. "Dozens of innocent babies were brutally murdered, and we're *debating* the merits? What ever happened to outright shame? Disgust? Anger? Is there anyone here who cannot see what's happening to the planet? We're dehumanizing the world!"

A quiet murmur rose, then faded among those seated at the table.

"Someone has to act." Jason continued. "And that someone might as well be me. I have started a new organization, the Gatestrian Knights, an outline of which rests on the table in front of you. This organization will cover the planet, empowering the local populations to take up the fight against evil, establish schools to teach children facts, not ideological fiction, and, most of all, instill the belief that innocent human lives are to be protected at any and all costs."

While those in attendance had an opportunity to skim through the booklet detailing the new organization, Jason poured himself a glass of water from the pitcher that sat near his chair, and took several sips before returning to his position in front of the large wall monitors.

"Terrorism, wars, economic upheaval. These are not our only problems." Jason continued. "Abortions, euthanasia, drugs. These have killed more people than any act of war or terrorism, but we have *socialized* the process. It's tolerable. It's sociable. It's expected!"

He walked over to another screen that showed a preview of a new television commercial. It showed a beautiful little girl with a voiceover that told the audience that her name was Maria, with her age of one year old blazoned in the background. The speaker went on to say "You wouldn't kill her now, why would you kill her then?" as the image shifted abruptly to an in-womb image of the little girl with her age listed as sixteen weeks, followed by a black screen with the words: ABORTION IS WRONG, DEAD WRONG.

"We will show this commercial in all markets at all times." continued Jason. "But this is not our only activity. We will be giving out millions in scholarships for impoverished children to attend Catholic schools, whether they are Catholic or not. We will have agents attend these schools, churches, everywhere to ensure that they uphold the faith."

Jason walked back towards his chair and sat down, resting his forearms on the large table. "In short, people, we will be *enforcing* the culture of life, not just preaching it. If an atheist says that they don't believe in God, so be it. If a Christian says, however, that abortion is a woman's choice, for example, then they will have hell to pay. We judge people by what they do, not who they are."

"Mr. Task." spoke an elderly woman seated several people away from Jason. "By what authority do we have the right to undertake such activities?"

"Ms. Wainwright." replied Jason. "By the same authority who will hold us accountable if we don't use the resources at our disposal to stop these atrocities."

"What you are proposing." spoke a man to the right of Virginia Wainwright. "Is vigilantism, is it not?"

"Mr. Van Allen." explained Jason. "Where there are laws, we work within the laws. Where there are no laws, we do what is necessary."

Jason rose up again, and walked towards the front of the conference room where the floor was raised up about two levels so that all would be able to see him clearly. "Listen, people. Any action that we will take pales in comparison with the implications of not taking any action. We cannot sit idly by and watch the world decay. Everyone of us has seen what happens in the war torn, depressed areas of the world where despots and gangs rule. It is no different than here in the so-called civilized world where the same butchery is merely institutionalized."

Pacing between the far corner and the center of the room, he continued. "We start schools, so that children will learn from the earliest ages that innocent humans are to be protected, that dignity requires morality. We develop a strong military so that we can move food and medical supplies into areas that are restricted by despotic regimes. And, we have our own people ensure that U.S. institutions are bound by the same code of moral standards that we govern ourselves by."

"What you are saying." spoke George Van Allen, Jason's deputy in charge of financial planning. "Is that we launch a war against the world?"

"No." reassured Jason. "We're going to launch a war against *evil*."

"Absurd." bellowed a gray haired woman from the back of the table.

"Absurd?" questioned Jason, pausing in his tracks. "Ms. Wilkinson, is it absurd to desire the destruction of evil within the world?"

"Mr. Task, may I ask how one strictly defines evil within the world?" challenged Martha Wilkinson.

"Easy." countered Jason. "Our adopted motto will be 'To protect the dignity and integrity of innocent human life, wherever and whenever it may be placed in jeopardy, and by whatever means may be necessary.' This is how we shall define evil – by anything that interferes with the foregoing."

"I see." retorted Ms. Wilkinson. "You define evil by *your* standards, by your laws, and deal with it via your methods."

"Ms. Wilkinson, as my political advisor, I respect your advice, but this is definitely not a political mission. People create politics, it is not a pre-existing thing. Life is. I, for one, do not care what the world thinks of me. I do not care which laws I violate. I want to defend life as I see it, punish those who are determined to destroy it, and basically do my damnedest to change this planet for the better. Any objections?"

The room became quiet, its occupants more focused.

"Good." replied Jason as he began to outline the inner workings of the Gatestrian Knights, and his plans for altering the world.

JACK STEPHENS STOOD at the podium in front of the eager reporters answering questions for the better part of an hour. He wished that he had ignored the request for a press conference, being somewhat fatigued from the long flight from Khartoum, but knew it was either answer the questions now or defend against accusations after they hit the front pages.

"Mr. Stephens." spoke a young redhead from the front row. "Bridget Jackson, Herald. Can you summarize the condition of General Kuraymahiyyun?"

"Well, Ms. Jackson. As you are aware, the general is now in custody at a secure location within Sudan. He's prepared to stand trial by a Sudanese court, overseen by the United Nations, European Union, and the Asian Conference. The general is in good shape, being treated well, and it will be a fair trial."

Jack pointed towards a black gentlemen in the back, a good friend of his. "Mr. Goshen?"

"Mr. Stephens, how do you answer charges that this was a most unethical and violent transformation of power? That you somehow had a hand in this brutal overthrow of a peaceful government?"

Jack smiled politely, entertaining thoughts of walking down the center aisle and bolo punching the reporter right out of his chair. "Mr. Goshen, all of this will come out in the trial. However, as for me, I would consider that any military leader who removes *his own government* from power is guilty of treason. That ordering the murder of thousands of people according to some fundamental difference – in this case, simply being Christian, is guilty of moral depravity. That anyone who orchestrates the torture and murder of innocent babies is guilty of nothing less than acute barbarism. No, Mr. Goshen, I wasn't involved with the removal of the general as proven by the fact that he is still alive and in one piece."

The group of reporters showed a little polite humor in their laughter, but few truly sided with Jack's line of thought. He guessed that ninety percent of the questions were negative towards him and the unknown parties who removed the general from power; nobody believing that the South Sudanese had the capability of conducting missions of such extraordinary response and effectiveness.

"Ladies and gentlemen." Jack spoke as he began to leave the podium. "I wish to thank you for the opportunity to set the record straight. I suggest, that you allow the courts time to review the case and provide appropriate justice. As for me, I shall continue my efforts to provide the Sudanese people with food, medicine, and other supplies. They are the ones who have suffered under the rule of this most brutal dictator."

Jack ignored a barrage of last minute questions and followed his security escort outside into the blazing Florida sun and into a waiting black Chevrolet Suburban which then whisked him away towards a waiting helicopter on the far end of Orlando International Airport.

He had been pleased with the relatively minor coverage of the Sudanese coup, an event whose fame had been overshadowed by a situation developing in Southeast Asia, between China and half a dozen other nations. Jack smiled to himself, the world was always willing to provide a trouble spot to take the attention away from a previous one. He couldn't have planned it better.

Still, Jack was worried about the Asian situation for he had several vessels operating within the region. Jason Task also had many tankers and gas carriers traveling the lanes and, as the future unfolded, what concerned one ultimately concerned the other.

For now, however, fortune favored them with the relative quiet that materialized out of Africa. Had the raid lasted for more than a single day, he knew, the situation would be far different. Even in today's technological age, things needed to be lengthy to sink into the public mindset. An event that lasted but a day, even a global shattering one, would not remain in the news if the public had no reason to read about it or view it.

Jack understood public perception. He also understood that the average citizen had the attention span of a two-year-old and the common sense of a teenager. A public trial of an entertainer would generate interest; the international trial of a deposed dictator wouldn't.

He looked out of the windows of the SUV as it sped around the airport on its way towards the helicopter field, coming to rest a short way from the white Bell Jet Ranger that only seconds before began warming up its engines.

Following his security team out of the Suburban, Jack hurried into the helicopter, more for motivation to get on with his vacation than as a desire to avoid more reporters or any would be assassin. As soon as he was securely within the aircraft, it rose up into the sky and began its run for Jack's Palm Bay estate.

ACROSS TOWN FROM the Task Tower sat an innocent looking white brick building with no windows and a small office facade consisting of aged clear glass and steel. Consisting of some four hundred and ten thousand square feet, the building's interior was anything but innocent in nature. This facility was Jason Task's advanced projects facility and contained more high-tech equipment than any other facility that he owned.

Known by its codename 'Crossword', the facility's function was to develop advanced technologies that could be used throughout the world by Tactical Extractions and, by extension, the Gatestrian Knights in their global pursuits. The EDS grenades, for example, which were used so effectively in Sudan were developed at this facility, as were the sensors on board the *SkyAction* series of spacecraft.

Perhaps somewhat unique within the military establishment, Crossword developed technologies that met the expectations and wishes of the troops in the field. Should any assault team member come up with an idea for an effective weapon, they could directly email the suggestion to the facility and, should the innovation prove effective, the product would be developed and implemented fully. In this regard, everyone was a design engineer in Jason's organization.

The financial rewards for innovation were widely understood, and great ideas meant great payoffs, so there was never a shortage of suggestions. Even techniques were rewarded with bonuses so for those who were great administrators instead of engineers could take advantage of Jason Task's generosity. In the end, however, great ideas meant saving lives and that's what everyone had on their minds whenever they did their jobs.

As normal, Jason arrived at the Crossword facility incognito – in this case traveling on a blue Harley, parking nonchalantly within the employee parking lot and not removing his helmet until he was inside the facility.

Here, things were less casual, with a smart looking receptionist as the sole indicator of business as usual. She politely waved at Jason and buzzed him through a locked door that permitted entrance into the main building. On the far side of the doors, however, *commercial* enterprise ceased and two armed guards holding automatic weapons greeted the executive who, as with everyone regardless of position, was patted down and scrutinized closely before being allowed to continue.

Walking down a short corridor, Jason stepped through a side door that led to an electronics fabrication and test facility, where he was greeted by a pale, tall man wearing a white lab coat over his suit.

"Dr. Brier." Jason reached out and shook the scientist's hand. "What marvels do you have today?"

Clarence Brier smiled. "A replacement for the EDS grenade."

"Oh?"

"Yes. It's quite fascinating. It looks like an ordinary rifle, but perhaps a bit wider."

"How does it work?"

"It transmits a laser beam that can detect an individual's heart resonance, analyze its signature, then transmit a pulsed electromagnetic beam that can neutralize that particular individual and nobody else."

"Remarkable."

"Yes, most remarkable."

Jason frequented the Crossword facility because he loved what was developed when he turned the best minds in the country loose. "What else do you have?"

"Well, Mr. Task. We're working on a new biopolymer-based armor plating that can stop .50-cal bullets and be only three millimeters thick."

"Wow."

"Yes, and it can be *sprayed* on."

"Woah. And it can stop .50-cal bullets?"

"Yes. Unfortunately, its not ready for body armor as of yet. I'm afraid that it does not adhere to any organic materials at the moment, but I am confident that we can solve that problem soon. Another problem is that it requires a static electric charge to function, and this is most difficult when the protected body is as complex as the human body is."

Jason nodded, following Brier into an adjacent room that served as a shooting range for small arms. "Now, what have you as far as lethal weapons?"

"We have improved our kinetic energy rifle. Its ammunition consist of small metallic disks that, upon electrical charge, explodes into the shape of a small projectile. The energy transferred in this conversion propels the projectiles out. This allows each soldier to carry a truly significant amount of ammunition as there is no explosive chemicals required."

Jason examined a prototype of the kinetic energy weapon handed to him by Brier. "It's larger than I expected, but well balanced. What's its penetrating power."

"It'll go through concrete and most armor. It'll make nice clean holes through soft tissue so I wouldn't recommend it on humans. With its speed of fire, it'll literally saw a soft body such as a human's in half within seconds. However, it would be exceptional against hard targets such as bunkers and tanks."

Jason handed the weapon back with reverence, then left the room to tour the vehicular assembly area, leaving Dr. Brier to attend to other projects.

The vehicular assembly area was a large manufacturing space devoted to the development of military and security vehicles and related subsystems. Its director was Dr. Bogdan Gritsenko, who warmly greeted his employer.

"Hello, Bogdan." Jason shook the engineer's hand. "*Как дела?*"

"Fine. Fine. I have many things to show you. Many things of which I am proud!"

The vehicular engineer led Jason to a corner of the plant with the enthusiasm of an expectant father and uncovered a small vehicle about the size of a subcompact car. It had no windows, and barely discernable tires.

"This is our autonomous combat vehicle." Gritsenko boasted with pride. "This vehicle can travel anywhere, under virtually any conditions, and take on anyone. All without human interdiction!"

"Really?" Jason's mind flashed to images of Hollywood science fiction movies, bringing him a little suspicion along the way. "You're not pulling one over on me are you?"

"No, sir!" Bogdan Gritsenko didn't hide the fact that he felt like he had been seriously insulted. "This vehicle can perform, however, it's still a prototype and too expensive to commit to battle. Yet."

"When will it not be too expensive?"

"Probably several more years. As it stands, it would have a survivability ratio of seventy-five percent. I wouldn't commit it until we get it to at least ninety-five percent."

"Get it to ninety-five."

"We are working most aggressively on this."

"If this thing does precisely what you say it can do, then pull out all of the stops. I'll provide you the development funds, out of my pocket if necessary."

"Then we will get it deployable."

"Can you create something similar for use on water?"

"We already have something in the works. It's being tested right now, or else I would be able to show it to you."

"Good." Jason shook his friend's hand, remembering the day that they first met when he rescued Bogdan from then Soviet Russia. "Listen, we're going to need a hell of a lot of advanced weaponry for our forces. Prime stuff. Keep up the good work and give us the things that they'll need. Let your imagination run wild and don't worry about funding. I'll figure something out."

14

AS GLOBAL TROUBLE spots go, the Spratly Islands of the South China Sea are a masterpiece, contested by no less than China, Malaysia, the Philippines, Taiwan, and Vietnam. None of the islands, which, depending upon one's definition of island could number in the hundred's, account for anything more than a mere rock jutting up out of the sea.

In strictly geopolitical economic terms, however, the islands represent something truly substantial, an extension of a nation's Exclusive Economic Zone and the opportunity to control vast amounts of offshore oil, natural gas, and subsea minerals. One such rock, barely distinguishing itself as nothing more than a navigational hazard, could conceivably extend a sovereign nation's territory by up to two hundred nautical miles.

Such convergence of national pride, wealth, and territory does not necessarily breed cooperation and trust, and the five claimants were all guilty of activities, overt and covert, designed to solidify their legal claim to the islands as a whole, with China and Vietnam leading the pack.

Aside from vast petroleum reserves, the Spratly Islands laid claim to another fact that served to intensify their role as one of the world's foremost trouble spots – they resided smack in the middle of one of the world's busiest shipping lanes. Virtually every type of vessel imaginable sailed through their waters with Singapore occupying one end and Taiwan and Japan the other.

Such valuable traffic also breeds another delectable recipe for disaster: piracy. The equatorial end of the South China Sea is arguably the world's most pirate infested waters and no ship, regardless of size, is immune from these ambitious if sometimes unrealistic hordes.

This was just such the environment that the Panamanian-flagged *Orient Task* sailed through regularly on its run from the gas fields of Qatar to its destination of Tokyo, carrying 137,000 cubic meters of liquefied natural gas.

The two hundred and seventy-six meter long vessel sailed from the Persian Gulf into the Indian Ocean, rounded Sri Lanka at twenty-one knots and headed for Indonesia where it slowed for its turn south through the Straits of Malacca near Singapore.

Having navigated the troublesome corridor of the Straits, it turned its ninety-three thousand ton bulk northwards and accelerated to twelve knots into the congested portion of the South China Sea, once again accepting commands from its autopilot.

With navigational duties well behind them, most of the fifty-five man crew on board the sea green colored *Orient Task* turned in for a decent night's sleep, leaving only an engineer and deck officer in charge of their safety. This was the ship's forty-seventh voyage, and its computer-aided navigational system had always performed brilliantly, with only an off season typhoon delaying their sixteenth voyage by a matter of two days.

Third Officer José Peña searched ahead through his Nikon binoculars, but could not see any lights beyond the bow of his massive tanker and instead turned his attention to the hundred mile radar which returned the echoes of the Spratly Islands ahead, at the scope's outer perimeter.

It was a quiet night, fewer vessels to be encountered than normal, and the seas exceptionally calm. Passage would be made to the west of Vanguard Reef, then Fiery Cross Reef which would take the large vessel no closer than one hundred nautical miles of the Islands. Like clockwork, Peña always seemed to draw the midnight shift whenever they passed through this region, and the monotonous routine became an old friend of his.

He didn't mind, for the sea was a family tradition and he knew that his was a better way of life than that of his father who had been a fisherman from Mindanao, pecking out a living barely sufficient to feed their family of six.

José Peña was still single, though he had a sweetheart in Manila, and did very well on his salary, so what was not to like? He also enjoyed the seclusion of the night watch, preferring it to the boisterous days when the skipper was present and everyone couldn't relax.

The fact that his vessel was carrying an extremely explosive cargo, one that could easily destroy an entire port, didn't faze him the least. In his opinion, it was still better than a desk job where the scenery never changed. The sea, he knew, never retained the same temperament.

Aside from the numerous small islands and reefs, as well as the occasional ship, José also had to be weary of the offshore oil platforms that began to creep up during the course of the past few years. Like islands, however, these facilities were fixed and located in precise locations that were easily marked on navigational charts.

Tonight, however, the only discrepancy in his otherwise monotonous routine was the small vessel that had been tailing his ship for the past two hours. Its blip on the radar screen indicated that it was nothing more than a small yacht, or perhaps fishing vessel, and stayed a precise one thousand meters behind.

On another night, perhaps, he would've established a brief chat with the following vessel, to remark about the weather, or the navigable duties surrounding the upcoming Big Bear and Blue Dragon oil fields, or any number of other subjects that mariners frequently find the need to discuss, but today José was a little hoarse, and didn't feel like placing any undue strain on his throat.

So, for lack of better options, he imagined what sort of vessel that it was that trailed his own ship. Too small for another LNG carrier, *way too small*. Could've been a small freighter, but ones this small were generally coastal vessels and wouldn't be out here. Might've been a small patrol vessel, sometimes they were as thick as flies – during the day. He concluded that it was probably a small Japanese fishing vessel on its way home from the Indian Ocean.

Strangely, he noticed, the vessel seemed to be making headway against his larger vessel's position while its blip simultaneously reduced in size. It couldn't have been a problem with the radar set; everything else seemed to remain where it was supposed to be. No, the small vessel was indeed picking up speed. No doubt about it. Twelve, maybe fifteen knots or more. Nothing significant, but noticeable just the same.

José left the orange glow of the bridge for a peek towards the stern, stepping outside on the starboard wing as he hoisted the pair of binoculars to his face. He saw nothing, no sign whatsoever of the vessel that trailed in their wake.

Walking back into the bridge, he immediately went over to the radar screen and scrutinized its image. Everything was there, including the mysterious vessel abaft. Strangely, the blip showed to be slightly west of where it had been before, but apparently it was not gaining as fast as it had been, or appeared as large.

Puzzled, he contemplated waking the captain, but decided to allow himself a few more minutes before he would sound any alarms.

ROBERTO HERNANDEZ WALKED onto his new teak balcony which overlooked the brilliant white sand beach and gazed out into the turquoise sea, pondering the email that he had just received on his Dell laptop. It was a detailed message outlining his role in a new organization called the Gatestrian Knights and informed him that he would be operating under the tightest level of secrecy and his primary mission would be the protection of innocent lives.

He largely ignored this directive – same old procedure, different name. Roberto had been hearing rumors through the grapevine that Jason Task would be expanding his operations into the politico-social arena and he concluded that this was just the formalization of this function.

It was the footer at the end of the email message that concerned him most, however. In amongst other, largely routine announcements regarding their activities, was a rather innocuous statement that the *Orient Task* had missed a daily check-in call.

Such events do not necessarily require disastrous explanations, but Roberto had been in the right place at the right time to perhaps shed some light on the whereabouts of the tardy ship. In fact, it was a tremendous amount of light that brought his attention to the subject.

Very early in the morning, while in the process of opening a bedroom window to his beachfront home in which to let in more tropical air, he noticed a brilliant light appear towards the southwest of Palawan. He could not, at that precise moment, ascertain the cause of the light.

Later, during breakfast, as he sat on his porch listening to the shortwave radio, he overheard fishermen speaking of a tremendous sound, as if from a large thunderstorm, but there was no such weather in the region at the time. Roberto had connected the dots and assumed that the light and the thunder were part of the same event and could only be construed as coming from an explosion of some sort.

Having considered all plausible theories ranging from naval activity to meteors, he couldn't come up with a sound explanation and this is where his interest sat until the mentioning of the *Orient Task*. His detective background immediately informed him that a large LNG tanker, fully loaded, constituted one hell of an explosive potential should the proper initiating agent be applied. What precisely would've torched off this explosion was anyone's guess, and it was this basic uncertainty that prevented him from contacting the vessel's operator until he could sort through the facts.

Roberto Hernandez was Tactical Extraction's senior investigator for Southeast Asia, having provided many years of thoughtful critique and consultation for Jason Task's regional exploits. Prior to that, he'd been a close confidant of Jack Stephen's since their Navy days. Now, he had learned, his services were being acquired by the Gatestrian Knights, though he was still fairly in the dark as to what his new role required of him.

For the moment, however, he was concerned with the delay in communications with the massive tanker and considering his employment, regardless of who ultimately signed his paycheck, wanted to see if he could provide an answer as to the whereabouts of the ship.

Walking back into his house, he headed immediately for his den where a large map of the region hung prominently from the wall. Using the bearing for the bright light that he witnessed, he traced the direction on the map and concluded that his hunch was correct, it originated within the direction that the vessel would've been traveling, though he had no idea of the distance involved.

On such a quiet, black night, the source of the light could've been far beyond the visual horizon, throwing off his analysis of the power of the explosion, its precise bearing, or even the exact time. Having only the hunch to work on, he concluded that the brilliant light, the thunderous sound heard by the fishermen, and the apparently missing vessel were all connected, and he set about to send a coded message to base operations.

All of this was mere formality, he knew, for if the *Orient Task* did in fact suffer a catastrophic explosion, it wouldn't have gone unnoticed. The explosive potential of a fully laden LNG carrier was akin to a small nuclear bomb and, quite incidentally, that's how he compared the brilliant light that he observed early in the morning.

Roberto spent his entire life as an investigator, first with the Navy, then as a civilian and he didn't need to wait around for orders. He was, after all, on a sizeable retainer as well as a steady paycheck so he could immediately set about carrying out his function without the necessity of waiting for funds to hire staff, purchase equipment, etc.

Today was no different, and he set about collecting his tools of the trade – his laptop, his satellite phone, his Sony digital camcorder, and his worn address book, among other things – so that he could initiate an investigation into the whereabouts of the presumed missing vessel and, most especially, its fifty-five crewmembers.

One fact had been sitting heavy on Roberto's soul; the last known position of the ship placed it squarely within the South China Sea from a run that took it through the Straits of Malacca. This placed the vessel in one of the world's most troublesome spots, with dozens of vessels of all sizes having been hijacked within the last decade alone.

Most of these events had been orchestrated by low-level pirates who had more in common with the Keystone Cops than a real threat, but the attacks within the region had slowly been developing in sophistication, particularly with the assaults against the larger tankers. Regardless, it didn't take a leap of the imagination to consider what might happen if an armed attack had been unleashed against the gas carrier.

Clad only in his red Hawaiian shirt, frayed white cut-off jeans, and sandals, Roberto concluded that he was sufficiently dressed to head into town and hopped aboard his moped for the short but time consuming drive to his office.

ANDRÉS MARTINEZ HAD been answering the damn telephone all morning as calls came pouring in regarding the massive explosion rumored to have taken the *Orient Task* down near the Spratly Islands. As the Forward Area Special Assistant for Tactical Extractions, he wasn't supposed to be even answering the telephone but his receptionist, Maria, was on her honeymoon and her replacement was at the dentist having a severely abscessed tooth removed.

Of all the blessed times to be alone at the office, he thought to himself, this was the worst. Fortunately, his sixteenth call, at least he *thought* it was his sixteenth, having lost all count hours ago, was from his supervisor Roberto Hernandez informing him that he was on his way to the office to help out.

Andrés scurried around the office collecting papers, regional action reports, intelligence estimates, and telephone leads, pausing for a moment to run his right hand through his thick black hair as he tried desperately to think of anything else that his boss might need.

He couldn't remember the last time he was so busy, and knew that he had never been involved in something so large and as unique as the whereabouts of a missing ship before. In fact, he concluded, he'd never been involved in something so *close* to their office – the last major event surrounding a North Korean missile launch.

For the most part, the small office on Palawan kept tabs on offshore oil activities within the South China Sea. Demanding, perhaps, but hardly full of intrigue. This, however, had the air of something different, something most unusual.

The first order of business whenever a ship went down was of course ascertaining its cause. Andrés ruled the weather out, navigational error as possible but unlikely and mechanical failure as equally remote. This left only hostile human intervention as a probable explanation.

He had just begun the long and tedious process of exploring this final option when he noticed Roberto's moped pull into the dirt parking lot and its unshaven, disheveled looking rider hop off and enter the building.

"Where's Julia?" questioned Roberto, somewhat confused as to the absence of people within the office.

"She's at the dentist." Andrés didn't have much time to explain such matters at the moment and dropped a stack of files onto a rickety desk, nearly toppling it over in the process. "I believe that you are aware that the *Orient Task* is missing, and we can pretty much rule out weather or groundings."

"Yes, yes." Roberto searched around for something to use as a desk, ignoring the mess. "I saw the light from the blast early this morning. It couldn't be anything but a catastrophic explosion of some sort. But what could've caused such a disaster?"

Andrés leaned forward to rest his bulk on a nearby table. "Any hostile activity that we know about?"

"Pirates, hijackers, drug runners...the usual."

"I've never known any to have attempted a strike against a gas carrier."

"Neither have I."

Andrés stood up straight; a thought flashed quickly through his mind as he grabbed a stack of files and began tearing through them.

"Remember something?" questioned Roberto, terminating his search for a place to sit down within the cramped office.

"I saw a report about suspicious Chinese naval activity in the area and I *thought* that it mentioned the presence of a submarine."

"A sub?" Roberto knew that it was a long shot, but the presence of a submarine could explain a lot of things regarding the mysterious circumstances involving the sudden loss of a massive LNG carrier. "It's probably just a coincidence."

Andrés nodded. "Still."

"Yes, I know. The Chinese have had it in for Jason Task ever since he started pushing religion into their country. But sinking a gas carrier?"

"I wouldn't put anything pass them." Andrés snorted. "I haven't trusted them since they held my father and 49 other fishermen back in January of 1988."

"Yes, I remember you telling me the story. The whole area of the Spratly Islands has left us with a powder keg ready to go off at any moment."

"Then would the destruction – accidental or otherwise – of a large ship be wholly unexpected?"

"No, I suppose that it wouldn't."

The two men searched throughout the office for the report indicating Chinese naval activity within the region during the past week, particularly the involvement of submarines but could not locate the file.

Roberto parked himself on the corner of Andrés' desk, contemplating the decision to send a message off to operations. "Hire us a helicopter." he spoke after several long minutes. "Let's fly over the area and see if we can find anything relating to the vessel's whereabouts."

"May I remind you." replied Andrés. "That the area is claimed by no less than five nations, a few of which may take exception to our nosing around."

"We have a legitimate need to be in the area as the vessel's representatives. We'd also be participating within the search and rescue missions. Nobody would be able to stop us legally."

"No, but they might give it an attempt if they're trying to cover up a hostile action against the vessel."

Roberto didn't buy the argument. He just felt uneasy with the thought that the Chinese navy had something to do with the loss of the ship, regardless of how well the theory flowed together. Still, he knew that other explanations such as mechanical failure or human error didn't pan out as well.

"Andrés, file a report with the main office. Mention the Chinese navy *only* as one possible explanation. Tell them that we're going to conduct a search of the area ourselves and to provide us with specific instructions as what to do next."

JASON SAT AT the conference table aboard his jet, poring over intelligence reports regarding recent activity within the South China Sea. Across the table from him sat a scale model of the sea green *Orient Task*, itself sitting atop a complete stack of vessel drawings and specifications.

Joining him on the flight to Singapore were several members of his Tactical Extractions group as well as salvage engineers and naval architects on temporary loan from Stephens Oceanographic. Most, however, had turned in for the night, leaving Jason alone at the large table contemplating his actions.

The loss of the *Orient Task* would set him back $300 Million, but it was the latest intelligence reports that fueled his concern. Unsubstantiated, but reliable nevertheless, reports had at least one survivor being picked up by a 'foreign' vessel, meaning that he could be in the possession of any one of the five or six nations that laid claim to the area.

Money could be recovered through insurance policies, but Jason truly valued his people, even if they were merely crewmembers who, working aboard ships, normally had a habit of changing assignments with the weather. It was a consistently reoccurring theme of his – let *everyone* know that he valued them.

He glanced up from his papers and stared at the model on the table, knowing that it wouldn't have taken much to send her to the bottom. An explosion in any one of her massive white tanks would've created a domino effect resulting in a solitary explosion of such immense proportions that nothing would remain of the large vessel.

Something that allowed even one survivor, however, would be rather unusual, indicating an initial blast far away from the cargo tanks. One survivor led credence to more survivors and hence the Tactical Extractions team that accompanied him on this flight.

The problem, however, concerned the slight suggestion of Chinese involvement within the report issued by Roberto Hernandez and Andrés Martinez stationed in Palawan. Jason knew that the Chinese maintained an aggressive presence in the area and experienced at least one major skirmish with every neighbor over the course of the past fifteen years.

Jason knew that the Chinese maintained a naval base at Fiery Cross Reef that included a meteorological and oceanographic research center, and they were building a second facility at Coffin's Nail Reef to the west. Of all the nations that fought over the islands, the Chinese, in his opinion, had the most at stake.

With crude passing the $60 per barrel mark and the substantial growth in its domestic needs, China needed to pad its coffers and what better place than somewhere where it already laid claim? Its main rival had been Vietnam and the two nations took jabs at each other for decades, with China ultimately developing an amphibious capability for its navy – just in case.

Jason wholeheartedly believed that such events as these were akin to Imperialist Japan's expansion during the period culminating with the Second World War, with much the same motivations. Like Japan then, China had to search outside of its territory for crude and, today, natural gas to fuel its booming economy.

As far as theories went, it was the most plausible but it still didn't explain the whereabouts of the vessel or its source of destruction. The former would be easy to ascertain, the latter required a significant amount of investigation, both of which involved Jason's tour of the area.

Intelligence traffic had indicated that something was brewing within the region, something that could escalate into a major international crisis. Several key factors within this area caused him no small amount of concern, compared with other locations that he had forces in.

For one, where there's oil there's international attention. While nowhere near as significant as the Middle East, Jason knew that the Spratly Islands region contained valuable oil concessions which could not be effectively exploited until the questions regarding ownership were settled. This in itself was a powerful motivator for an expansionist regime.

Secondly, China was no small operator. Although it did not have the technical prowess of, say, Soviet-era Russia, it did have a significantly more productive economy with the United States as one of its largest, if not *the* largest, trading partners.

While he had conducted operations within Chinese territory before, they were by no means history altering events. If China was involved in, and this was by no means certain, the disappearance of the *Orient Task*, Jason knew that he simply couldn't just go into Beijing and have it out with the Chinese government.

Jason reclined in his seat, knowing that this region had diplomacy's filthy hands all over it. First he would have to locate the vessel and determine the facts. Next, he would have to make his case to the international community. Then, he would have to wait until they decided what should be done, what could be done, and whether it *would* be done.

15

THE SUN'S RAYS lapped at the waves sending flashes of light hurling across the sea in a spectacle worthy of Neptune himself, as the salvage vessel *Miss Jamie IV* positioned herself directly above the wreckage, her dynamic positioning system keeping the vessel within a meter of her designated target.

Two thousand meters beneath the ship lay the remains of the *Orient Task*, having been discovered only three weeks earlier by the salvage crew currently on station.

"I never saw such wreckage." spoke Jason as he carefully viewed the computer screens that lined the desk in front of him. "To imagine such a large vessel reduced to scrap metal."

Jason stood within the robotics control center of the *Miss Jamie IV*, itself merely a portable trailer tied to the working deck of the salvage vessel. Here, he could witness the images coming in from the bottom, in real-time and without processing. It was a chance to become connected with the ship before analysts and computer programmers desensitized the evidence in the name of forensic investigation.

The color images that flowed in from the depths showed no hint of a ship; the video seemed to come from some subsea junkyard. Tattered pieces of metal lay strewn about the seafloor for a thousand meters in all directions, the heart stopping confirmation of a catastrophic explosion.

Jason's eyes were transfixed to the monitors even though he realized they were gazing upon the grave of so many fine men. That an explosion sent the once mighty ship to the bottom was a given.

What precisely caused such a powerful explosion, however, is what kept him awake at nights.

Piece after piece glided through their field of view and yet nothing was especially recognizable. True, the emotionless eyes of the trained engineer or naval architect could call out the presence of a bulkhead door, or a hatch, or a stern anchor, but such eyes are inadvertently attached to an emotional human soul which cannot recognize items in their impractical, passionless state.

Ninety-three thousand tons of wreckage scattered across four square kilometers of ocean bottom proved to be a daunting task for the search effort, and Jason quietly questioned their chances of success. He knew that they wouldn't have the luxury of retrieving every piece and reconstructing the vessel on land as if it had been an airliner disaster, but he further realized that any one piece could prove to be the key to the puzzle and so the photographic missions were carried on daily.

Billy Andersen, the ROV pilot on duty, massaged his sore eyes as he guided the miniature robot through the seemingly endless debris field. "My God, I haven't seen such destruction in all of my life."

"Neither have I." Jason answered to no one in particular. "Nowhere."

Billy brought the remotely-operated vehicle up slightly to pass over a chunk of metal that couldn't be identified before allowing the small robot to return to its normal depth. "Whatever that was, it looked like it had been melted."

"When was the last time that we found anything recognizable on this pass?" asked Jason.

"Hours."

"I don't even remember what it was."

"A chair, I *think*."

"Oh, yes."

Tilting the joystick to the right, Billy maneuvered the vehicle around another mass of metal, before straightening out its path. "It's a damn obstacle course down here."

Jason knew that another approach was needed, and thrust his body back in an effort to stretch his muscles, releasing his cognizant energy. "We need a wide-field survey so that we can pick out targets of interest before we go in close for a look-see."

The last salvage effort that Jason had to deal with concerned the loss of his ore freighter *William B. Channing* which went down in Lake Michigan. That vessel literally broke apart during a storm and it was discovered that the shipbuilder had used sub par steel in an effort to trim costs.

As horrible as the *Channing* disaster was – claiming all but three of its crew – that wreck was largely intact and the cause for the sinking was determined rather quickly. Here, however, the wreckage was scattered all over, and although the event of an explosion was a given, the initiator of the blast could've been a small item that vaporized in the process.

Jason, though quietly for fear of panic, hadn't ruled out a bomb either. The sinking of the *Orient Task* erupted onto the front pages back in the United States where many communities that had warmed to the prospects of locating LNG facilities in their regions now took up the crusade against them for fear that such an explosion could obliterate their towns.

As with the *Channing* disaster, however, help in the form of unsolicited theories and explanations poured in, ranging from the believable to such unbelievable events as alien abductions, lasers beamed from space, or time warps. The presence of such ridiculous people was one of the many reasons that he always managed to find himself in the field during an event such as this.

"Sir, I think that you should see this."

Jason leaned forward on the console to see what had caught Billy Andersen's attention. Barely visible within the camera's focus was a tubular structure with what seemed to be a pair of fins protruding from its sides.

"Sir." continued Billy quietly. "I've been on ships for years, and I've also been in the Navy. Yet, I don't ever recall seeing any fins like that, except for maybe on a missile or torpedo."

"Can't be." Jason couldn't accept the explanation. "A missile or torpedo would've been the one thing that was obliterated. There wouldn't be anything left to it!"

"Not necessarily. An explosive charge could've blown the aft section of the torpedo away from the vessel before all hell broke loose."

"It's got to be a coincidence." countered Jason, still disbelieving the theory proposed. "Mark the location so we can retrieve this thing for further analysis."

"Already done."

JOHN D. SAVAGE, the *Miss Jamie IV*'s senior marine engineer examined the peculiar device with the patience of a grandmother inspecting a loaf of bread at the corner market. "Fins? Yes. Torpedo? Probably. Chinese? Possibly."

"Get to the point." snapped Jason, ignoring the need for analytical thinking. "What the hell is this thing?"

Savage paused for several minutes as he tugged repeatedly at the fins protruding from the object. It was readily apparent that they were normally stowed within its body, and then sprang out upon firing. "If this is what I *think* it is, it's something truly extraordinary."

"Well, what the hell is it?"

"It could be a *Shkval* torpedo." Savage stopped his playing around with the device and spun around to speak directly to Jason.

"A what?"

"An underwater rocket. The Russian's have been developing it since the 1960's and rumor has it that the Chinese have purchased some of them."

"How does this *Shkval* thing work?"

"It's launched like a normal torpedo, coming out of the tube at about fifty knots. Then, its rocket engine ignites sending the vehicle forward at about two hundred and thirty knots."

"*Two hundred* and thirty knots?"

"Yes. It works through the process of supercavitation. Basically, a continuous stream of gas is discharged from the nose of the torpedo, running along its side and forming a type of anti-drag envelope that allows the vehicle to approach speeds unheard of for traditional torpedoes."

"And this thing actually exists?" Jason's lower lip disappeared underneath his upper teeth as he listened to the description of this advanced weapon.

"Oh, yeah. It was being developed to attack U.S. nuclear submarines which had better sonar than the Russians and, later, for use against large targets such as carriers. It was widely rumored that the lost of the *Kursk* had something to do with this weapon, but that might be stretching it."

"Wow. Something like that would be difficult to defend against. I mean two hundred and thirty knots!"

"It would be *impossible* to defend against."

"I'd sure as hell bet that it would be! And this thing was with the wreckage of the *Orient Task*?"

"Oh, that could simply be a coincidence, found by our search for the tanker. On the other hand, the speed at which these things travel, they make excellent kinetic energy weapons."

"Meaning?"

"Meaning that they don't need to possess an explosive warhead for them to do significant structural damage to a ship."

Jason sunk his chin into his right hand, forming a brace against his chest and thought long and hard about the implications. "Still, you shoot a pipe through a tanker, even at two hundred knots, and it wouldn't take the ship down fast enough to prevent a distress signal from going out or its survivors taking to the boats."

"No." agreed Savage. "I'm afraid that even with a warhead on board, it wouldn't account for the speed of destruction that's apparent within the scene that we've witnessed. Something had to cause a nearly instantaneous explosion of *all* five cargo tanks. Otherwise, there'd be witnesses, survivors, even floating debris. When this ship went, it literally blew itself to bits within seconds."

"But what?" Jason hated not having answers, especially to problems that seemed so obvious at first. Still, he realized that simply vaporizing a ship wasn't an easy thing to do. "John, if you were to take out a ship this fast, how would you do it?"

"Hell, Mr. Task. I haven't a clue. Sure, I could say 'Nuke the damn thing' but there wouldn't be any question about that. This ship simply exploded."

Jason nodded his head. "I'm going to have to contact my people back in the States and get a tech conference going or something. I need answers."

"DR. BRIER." SPOKE Jason as he saw the facial image from the Crossword facility appear on his computer screen. "I've got a problem and I need your help."

"Sure thing, Mr. Task." replied the always professional Clarence Brier.

"Do you know anything about a supposed rocket torpedo called a *Shkval*?"

"Sure, who hasn't?" replied Brier, going over the facts that Jason had learned only a few hours before.

"Apparently, I didn't." Jason tried to tame his embarrassment, but was more interested in gaining knowledge than admitting that he was in the dark about something. "At least, not until we found one."

"You *found* one?"

"Well, a part of what John Savage believes is one. Our problem, however, is how to explain the sudden destruction of the vessel from a simple torpedo hit, even if it moved as fast as these things are supposed to."

The image of Clarence Brier's face showed a deep concern for the problem, a contortion of the skin of someone whose thoughts ran back through the ages. "It might've not been merely a simple torpedo, even if it was a rocket propelled one."

"What's on your mind?"

"Well, for the sake of argument, let's conclude that it was a *Shkval* torpedo and launched by a Chinese submarine."

"Okay."

"Now, the question remains, what caused the ship to literally vaporize. First, the Chinese are good at taking other people's products and improving them. For example, their first manned spacecraft is basically a copy of the Russian *Soyuz*. Now, if they were spending a fortune building their new Type 093 nuclear attack submarine and wanted something special to equip it with, wouldn't they be inclined to take the latest technology available and expand upon it?"

"Perhaps. It saves money."

"Yes. The Russians have the technology and the Chinese have the money. Now, here's what I'm getting at. Suppose, just suppose, the Chinese mate a *Shkval* torpedo with some form of electromagnetic warhead. It could unleash an electrical discharge that could just provide enough of a spark to detonate one or more of the cargo tanks."

"Hmm." Jason thought about the EDS grenades that served so well in Sudan. "Just how powerful a charge could be imparted upon the vessel?"

"Theoretically speaking, as large as you would like. However, it needn't really be all that big. A simple static discharge could blow the tanks. After all, you've already got *potential* in the form of an extremely cold liquid fuel; you cool a flammable gas to several hundred degrees below zero and you've got all the earmarks for a static induced explosion *without* the need for an external initiator."

"True, but why attack a LNG carrier in the first place?"

"Maybe it's just the shear sophistication of the ship? After all, it's nearly the size of an aircraft carrier. It possesses the latest in fire and safety gear, not to mention navigation and communications equipment. Plus, if properly achieved, it would go down without much evidence."

The lump in Jason's throat exploded into his stomach. "Just like the condition of the wreckage."

"Yes, precisely."

"Okay, so we have a theory. It's still just a theory, right?"

"Yes. One that does, however, explain a lot of circumstantial evidence. First, you have a LNG carrier go down within minutes near several Chinese navy bases; themselves part of a hotly contested region. Second, you find what amounts to be a super secret weapon amongst the debris field. Third, the Chinese government has spent a fortune developing just such technologies to enhance its global status."

"And, for lack of better words, the Chinese government doesn't like me very well."

"That too." Clarence Brier chuckled at the thought. "But then again, that would implicate a sizeable portion of the planet."

"Yeah." Jason knew Brier was correct on all accounts, but it still didn't permit conviction for the crime. "Given all of this, how would you suggest going about the investigation?"

"First, you'd have to go about increasing your intelligence. Find out who's been operating in the area at the time, what equipment they've been using, and who's got the motive. Then, you have to pay them a visit and see you if can trace the equipment directly to them without relying upon hearsay. "

"Great!" retorted Jason. "Suppose it *is* the Chinese. We can't simply just go snooping around their country for answers."

"You might be able to find what you're looking for at one of their bases in the Spratly Islands. They're pretty unguarded considering all of the activity that's being conducted there lately."

"Perhaps, but you'd better start working on some technologies to give us an edge."

"Anything in particular that you want?"

"We'll need to eavesdrop on their military conversations, so some good communications equipment."

"We have those already stored and ready to ship. Should have them to you within a day or two."

"Good. Also, as we'll *probably* be tangling with the Chinese of all people, we'll need some adequate firepower. Not just rifles and machine guns."

"Right."

"Lastly, there's about a hundred or so damn islands down here, if you want to call them that. We'll need some high performance boats that can skim over shallow reefs and still be large enough to provide protection and fire support for our teams."

"We can ship the *Sea Tigers* down; they're ready."

"Good, good. But spice them up a little with some of your latest hardware. We must, I repeat must, be able to handle any activity down here."

"I understand."

"*Somebody* down here destroyed a half billion dollar ship and cargo, and I have fifty-five men missing. I want the bastards to pay, regardless of who committed the crime. I am hereby instructing you to send us everything that you have or can have available within a reasonable amount of time, regardless of cost. I am executing Directive Corduroy."

"Yes, sir. I understand fully."

16

ROBERTO HERNANDEZ NERVOUSLY went about providing refreshments for his guests, an event that was supposed to have taken place at his office instead of his home, but with the addition of more arrivals, he had no alternative.

Not only was the esteemed Buenaventura Ramos there, but also Jason Task – *everyone's* boss – and his wildest imagination couldn't comprehend the status of these two great men, nor of the situation that had found them setting together within his tiny beachfront home.

Andrés Martinez had been briefing the group on the status of Chinese submarines known to have been working throughout the region, especially from their Coffin's Nail Reef base, which Beijing vehemently denied even existed.

"As you gentlemen are aware." Andrés spoke, relying on notes written on a stack of multicolored 3x5 index cards which he flipped through his hands quickly. "The Chinese Type 093 nuclear attack submarine just became operational, replacing the Type 091 *Han* Class. The Type 093 is about the same size as the Russian *Victor III* class – still a major advancement for the Chinese Navy – and displaces around 6,500 to 7,000 tons. It has a pressurized water reactor coupled to a single, asymmetrical seven bladed skewed propeller."

Andrés took a sip of his tropical drink before continuing his narration. "The submarine can carry both wire-guided and wave-homing torpedoes, as well as anti-ship cruise missiles, anti-submarine missiles, mines, and possibly land attack cruise missiles."

"In short, it can conceivably carry anything the Chinese have in their arsenal?" Jason asked, still electing to withhold the information regarding the new rocket torpedo.

"Yes, sir." replied Andrés. "They experienced difficulty in developing the Type 093, mainly with radiation shielding and noise reduction, which might've explained the recent modifications to the Type 091 class. However, they are expected to have at least six submarines operational by 2012."

"Do you know whether it was a Type 091 or a Type 093 that was near Fiery Cross Reef when the *Orient Task* met its fate?" questioned the dignified Buenaventura Ramos.

"No sir." Andrés' nervousness was elevated more by the presence of Ramos than by that of the much more powerful Jason Task. Ramos had achieved an almost cult-like admiration among Filipinos for his role in combating Islamic terrorists on Mindanao. "Unconfirmed sources tend to lean towards a Type 093, but we have no way of knowing for certain."

"Gentlemen." Jason walked over towards the front of the group, the debate over the *Shkval* torpedo still flowing through his mind. "I am under the impression that it was a Type 093. I base this conclusion upon the nearness of several secretive Chinese bases, as well as the finding of a rather extraordinary weapon system that we uncovered during the search through the wreckage site. What I want to know now is, can we determine from which base the Chinese are inclined to operate Type 093's?"

"They could use Fiery Cross Reef." interjected Roberto, completing his task of providing refreshments to the group. "But there are too many non-military people around there."

"There are as many as eight other bases in the region." added Andrés, confirming the thought with his notes.

"While the information is strictly circumstantial." replied Ramos. "I believe that we are dealing specifically with China. Ever since the breakup of the Soviet Union which removed a threat from the north, the Chinese have pushed their intentions southward, towards the South China Sea.

"They've moved *Kilo*-class submarines into the area, attempted to purchase an aircraft carrier from Ukraine, and are very forthright about creating a blue-water, naval arm of the People's Liberation Army.

"Moreover, Beijing has based a rapid-response force on Hainan Island in order to defend their claims within the Spratly Archipelago, which as you are aware, is a territory of historical significance for the Chinese people and one in which there's a great deal of national pride to protect."

"*Gracias Señor* Ramos." Jason had heard enough; he now firmly believed that the Chinese were the culprits behind the sinking. "We have, in our possession, evidence that the Chinese may have been involved. During our search of the debris field, we located the remains of a *Shkval* torpedo.

"Such a weapon system could've contained a form of warhead – an electromagnetic warhead – that could've have caused the tanks on board the *Orient Task* to explode. The question that remains concerns whether the torpedo's presence within the debris field was coincidental or not."

"Perhaps it wasn't." replied Andrés. "My sources spoke of a new Chinese test scheduled for the region during the week that the *Orient Task* ultimately went down. I remember it because the source specifically stated that the test was delayed because the production of a submarine was running behind schedule from the previous year."

"Gentlemen." Jason spoke calmly. "We're going to have to uncover facts regarding whether the Chinese do have *Shkval* torpedoes in their possession, and whether such weapons are in use by the vessels within the South China Sea."

Everyone present knew precisely what Jason meant; they were going to have to provide physical evidence and this meant going into Chinese territory and either photographing or otherwise removing technological evidence.

Unlike the lightning raid into Khartoum, which intelligence showed to the be current location of the despotic general, there was no such intelligence providing clues as to whether the Chinese were involved or whether they actually had the weapon which was found within the wreck site.

THE FREIGHTER *ARAFURA Sea Paradise* sailed north of the Natuna Islands, near the northern limits of recognized Indonesian territory, slowly making its way towards the Spratly Archipelago.

Winds had picked up from the south, but were nowhere near threatening and the sun had just made its presence known in the east, throwing up a bouquet of oranges, yellows, and quickly disappearing indigos.

Deep within the hold of the cargo vessel laid six sinister looking watercraft – high speed assault vessels tailored specifically for raids against hardened shore facilities. These were the *Sea Tigers*, the much modified boats frequently used by Tactical Extractions to patrol waterfront sites and other vessels.

The pale gray and cobalt blue assault craft, twenty meters in length, could maintain a cruise speed of fifty knots with dash speeds approaching nearly eighty. Their multi-faceted hull provided an exceptional stealth capability while the newly added kinetic energy disc gun occupying the forward deck could launch 20mm projectiles at a rate of ten thousand rounds per minute, unleashing a deadly volley against any target.

Mixed in with the cargo of deadly attack boats were containers of advanced communications systems, small arms, ammunition caches, fuel barrels, and field rations. The presence of such dangerous cargo meant that the *Arafura Sea Paradise* had to avoid most ports of call, having recently fueled at a secure location within Thailand.

The mission of the old and reliable freighter, of course, was not to simply visit ports of call, but to serve as a mother ship for the assault vessels that it delivered to the world's trouble spots. It was a floating command post, maintenance center, and amphibious embarkation point all rolled into one.

Based in Guam, the U.S. flagged *Arafura Sea Paradise* took a little over two weeks to reach its current position, having first waited two weeks for the cargo which it carried to arrive from the mainland.

Every man on board knew the role for which the vessel served – they couldn't escape noticing the unique cargoes and destinations – and everyone of them volunteered for the duty. For their loyalty and capability, they were among the best paid mariners on the planet, even if the vessel didn't overtly raise the subject.

The *Arafura Sea Paradise* was an older vessel, not quite drawing the attention from any ports that she did visit, but this was strictly for appearance sake. To be neither inviting nor challenging permits a vessel from being inspected by those who may take delight in discovering her true cargo.

While her outward appearance may have seemed somewhat mediocre, her internal facilities were proud and served her crew well. They had to, for she sailed longer routes than would be normally considered and therefore her crew would serve longer and be away from shore amenities for greater durations.

None of this seemed to concern the crew, for they often took pride in reading about some mysterious event which happened at some dangerous location and knew that they had a small role in the affair, having delivered the equipment needed to undertake such efforts.

To know that it may all come crushing down should the true nature of the vessel's cargo be discovered provided something of a rush that no amount of money could. Her crew were risk takers, but they were *calculated* risk takers who would never jeopardize either themselves or the ship for glory's sake, preferring to retain confidence in the overall mission.

Captain Gerald Davis was no exception to this rule, having sailed direct to Thailand to present the appearance of loading cargo in order that suspicion would not be raised regarding a vessel that retreated in mid-ocean for no apparent reason. This act added a week to her sailing schedule but offered the pretense of a normal freighter carrying out normal functions.

A chess player in his off time, the silver-haired, chiseled jaw Davis orchestrated every move as if it was another game, albeit one with higher stakes. It kept his aging mind nimble, his ship safe, and his crew alive.

In certain ways, the *Arafura Sea Paradise* was just a modern, more or less private, version of the deepwater vessels that served during the Normandy invasion of World War II. She would reach a selected destination, hoist the small attack boats up through the cargo opening with her cranes, pivot, and lower them alongside the side where their crews could climb in before lowering them to the water.

Furthermore, the ship needn't have stopped for all of this to take place, and many missions have been conducted via the cover of darkness, and anyone spying the larger vessel with radar would not detect any major differences in her operation.

First Mate Wilson Smith and Boatswain John Monroe were in charge of the deployment of the attack vessels and knew their job well. Smith handling the administrative and operational duties of ensuring that each boat had the correct equipment assigned for its mission, and that each crew was provided with up-to-date navigational information regarding their region. Monroe, for his part, ensured that the physical condition of the boats was sound, as well as that their launching was carried out without any problems.

Whenever the chance allowed – and this was something that didn't happen very often – drills would be conducted at sea with all six boats launched to carry out a makeshift mission such as to sink a floating barrel or photograph a group of whales then retrieved and stowed before anyone saw what was going on.

Under exceptional conditions, all six *Sea Tiger* boats could be deployed inside of half an hour. During adverse weather conditions, such deployment would take a hour or longer. Fortunately, for the attack boat crews, the *Arafura Sea Paradise's* operational area ensured favorable weather most of the time.

JASON TASK SAT within the main salon of the motor yacht *Sanctity* as it drifted casually within the Sulu Sea just east of Palawan. The elegant and traditional yacht served as his floating command center and heliport, as well as provided him with a home away from home during his oceanic expeditions.

Save for, perhaps, her landing pad, a casual observer might've mistaken her for a representative of the golden age of trans-Atlantic steamships, never minding the fact that the immaculate white vessel was less than four years old.

Well-equipped for her role as floating office, Jason often used her for vacations, enabling him the flexibility of solitude while still maintaining quick access to his empire should the need arise. In effect, she served as the waterborne version of his Jagged T Ranch, and both held the same special place within his heart.

Today, however, was by no means a vacation and the reams of intelligence reports that sat in front of him drove home the point. He had no less than ten reports that Chinese Type 093 nuclear submarines had been pulling into their secretive Coffin's Nail Reef base. More disturbing, was the indication that these deployments had something to do with a new anti-ship weapon.

If this circumstantial evidence didn't point towards the Chinese as the culprits who sank the *Orient Task*, one remaining and largely overlooked fact did – the large LNG carrier was built in Taiwan, the perennial sore point for Sino-International relations. It might've been merely a coincidence, but Jason couldn't accept it as such, and from the moment on, all information contained an element of prejudice in his planning, a prejudice, however, that turned out to be valid.

Key among the evidence were reports that China sought ways in which to destroy naval vessels without revealing trace evidence as to who had actually carried out the destruction. Another report contained instructions from Beijing regarding a policy of blaming other nations for certain events.

Jason began to believe that China had a role in the destruction of his ship but wanted to blame another nation for its sinking for as of yet unknown political reasons. If this were true, then the use of a *Shkval* torpedo armed with an electromagnetic-type warhead would definitely serve its purpose.

From a historical perspective, the information he reviewed seemed to fall in line. Sino-Vietnamese relations, for example, were frequently heated as Vietnam had no military powerful enough to ward off Chinese aggressions. To counter this reality, Hanoi had been making friendly overtures towards the United States which Beijing wanted to disrupt at all costs.

Practically everything the Chinese did reflected a foreign policy based on expansionist ambitions and any nation that sought to contain these goals was considered by Beijing as a threat. Because of this view, the communist government was in fact dominated by the powerful People's Liberation Army which sought to propel the nation into superpower status.

After spending several hours reading the intelligence reports, Jason envisioned a plausible theory regarding the destruction of the gas carrier, one that might warrant an indictment if not a conviction were he to take the case to a court of law.

He believed that Chinese expansionism, mandated by a need for petroleum and other natural resources, elevated the Spratly Archipelago dispute to the fore of its foreign policy activities, which placed Beijing squarely on the opposite side of the fence with its neighbors which generally maintained close ties with the United States.

To challenge this alignment, China had decided to implicate another party – possibly Vietnam – in an event which would, undoubtedly, create tensions between the United States and the scapegoat. By singling out the *Orient Task* as the target, Beijing could realize several practical and cultural objectives.

First, by attacking the gas carrier, they could test out the newly purchased *Shkval* torpedoes as well as the performance of their much delayed Type 093 attack submarine. Secondly, because the *Orient Task* was built in Taiwan and insured through the government in Taipei, this problematic nation would bear the brunt of the financial loss, which gave the mainland Chinese government a cultural jab against those preaching independence.

Lastly, the destruction of the *Orient Task* would have given the People's Liberation Army an opportunity to test a new weapon that could help prepare it to ultimately take on the dominant power in the region – the United States – all at the expense of another nation.

Jason had one final piece of the puzzle to locate. He had to find proof that the Chinese did in fact possess the *Shkval* torpedoes. His intelligence analysts had documented that Russia had sold the weapons to China. All that was required now was proof that the weapons were in *Chinese* hands. Given this confirmation, it would be a very small leap to suggest that the torpedo that lay amongst the ship's wreckage could've only come from a Chinese vessel because Russian vessels were not operating in the area at the time of the tanker's destruction.

What Jason really wanted, was to prove that the torpedo that was recovered from the site came from the same batch that the Russians sold them, thereby providing an *exact* set of dates that could match the time of the sinking. Reluctantly, however, he had to make his decisions solely on circumstantial evidence.

The knowledge that the raid in Khartoum had been carried out with lightning rapidity and minimal casualties across the board did little to ease Jason's mind. China was not Sudan, and even if Coffin's Nail Reef was hardly more than a rock stuck within the middle of the ocean, Beijing *had* the wherewithal to launch a major counterstrike against his assets.

His ultimate dream of creating a truly global organization to save the world could once again be snuffed out of existence by a single nation whose reputation made it *the* antithesis of the Gatestrian Knights. Equally unsettling was the fact that if the Gatestrian Knights were to succeed as he imagined it, it would have to be able to deal directly with such threats as the Chinese government.

Given enough time and money, he was well aware, he could achieve anything. Unfortunately, money was governed by practicality and time was the sole domain of God; Jason knew that if war was to come, he would have to fight it with what he had available and not what he wanted.

His best strategy was to survive long enough until he could gain dominance, either by wealth, technology, or shear luck. Only with technology could he expect to have some control, and this is where he placed a significant portion of his assets. Luck, he decided, would be accepted as it happened.

17

APPROXIMATELY ONE HUNDRED and fifty nautical miles west of Fiery Cross Reef, abutting the 200 meter depth boundary of the Spratly Archipelago, Coffin's Nail Reef – renamed *Ling Mu Jiao* by the Chinese – stood as hardly more than a V-shaped shoal anchored by a tiny island at its apex.

From any distance, one would be hard pressed to spot the tiny speck of land were it not for the concrete structures that rose up from the island and the three hundred meter long pier that split the shoal and allowed vessels of all types to dock and unload supplies or receive maintenance support from the base's twenty man staff.

During the day the miniscule base baked underneath the near equatorial sun, the few palm trees providing virtually no shade with which to cool oneself. During the night, it disappeared into the blackness of the South China Sea, experiencing nature's camouflage at its best.

Life was boring on the tiny little outpost without much beyond a simple poker game or some other much frowned upon activity to entertain the staff. Port visits by ships were few and far between, and only served to jar the lives of the staff, who more often than not, had to dress proudly in their military uniforms forsaking any chance for comfort.

This disruption in their daily life was compounded whenever the visitor was a nuclear submarine such as the bold, new *Zhan shi*, which could increase their population fourfold. Fortunately for the island's inhabitants, the crews of the submarines were nearly always restricted to the vessel for security purposes – an order that the submariner's never questioned once they themselves learned of the facilities that the base offered.

Being charged with their duties at Coffin's Nail Reef for two-year stretches, the staff became somewhat less Chinese in certain ways before their departure and many would volunteer to remain at their forcibly adoptive home, a decision that the naval administrators in Beijing were more than willing to oblige.

For their part, the crews of the nuclear submarines considered their island based brethren as belonging to something of a lower class, virtual throwbacks to the age of dinosaurs and caveman. Assignment to a modern nuclear submarine was a highly competitive procedure, whereas assignment to *Ling Mu Jiao* often entailed nothing more strenuous than a simple request.

Because of this, a great deal of subversive hostility percolated between both groups and often degraded the quality of maintenance provided to the visiting submarines. Often, workers were only permitted to the vessels under armed guard, and even then things didn't always go as planned.

Over time, the island's misfits realized that poor quality led to the inevitable return of the submarine and their attention to detail increased if only for the purpose of preventing the *nán zǐ qì* crews of the nuclear subs from spoiling another day.

This period of *détente* between the two opposing factions was in full force when the *Zhan shi* limped into Coffin's Nail Reef after experiencing a cooling pump failure in her reactor, forcing the submarine's commander to initiate an unscheduled stop. The repair order simply stated that the cause for the failure was due to "severe underwater concussions experienced during Training Mission One Two Nine."

Without the use of the cooling pump, the submarine's nuclear reactor would have to be shut down for a period of three days while a replacement pump was installed, forcing the vessel to power up its emergency diesel generator. So, for the next thirty-six hours the uniforms went on, the poker decks went into lock-up, and the tiny, remote island became Chinese again.

BOATSWAIN JOHN MONROE paced the deck, barking out orders that the crew swore could be heard deep within hostile territory. "Lower Boat Five! Damn you, Allen! I told you not to get in the way!"

Assistant Boatswain Maurice Allen ignored the bitching, he had done his job hundreds of times before and any alteration in his methods was justified by the unique situation imposed by every mission. "It's the damn turnbuckle! It's corroded or something!"

Monroe stormed over to Davit Five and slapped Allen lightly against the back of his head. "Listen here, Mo-reese! There's nothin' corroded on *my* ship! The trick of the matter is to use your hands and *turn* the goddamn thing!"

The ever alert boatswain didn't hang around long enough to see if Number Five Boat was lowered as he marched across the deck to the starboard side to check on Number Two Boat's progress.

"Web-BER!" roared Monroe as he observed the boat being lowered halfway down the side. "Make sure the crew is in the boat *before* you send it down!"

"Gosh, Monroe!" replied Weber Krantz, the ship's Second Assistant Boatswain, trying his damnedest to count heads in the dark. "They were in ten minutes ago!"

"No excuses!" John Monroe never let his men believe for a second that they were doing their jobs properly; he always informed them that there was plenty of room for improvement. "If they were in ten minutes ago, then how come they are *still* here?"

Wilson Smith looked at his watch and shook his head softly. It was the third time that the first mate glanced at the timepiece in the last five minutes. "Twenty minutes and only three of the boats are in the water. We must work faster."

"Monroe's never been late so far." Captain Davis covered his mate's wristwatch with his hand. "You'll go out of your mind if you keep looking at that damn thing. I'm going to the bridge, let me know when all boats are underway."

"Yes, sir." Smith took another compulsory peek at the watch as the skipper left for the bridge. *C'mon, Monroe. Get those bastards in the water.*

Within another ten minutes, all six assault boats were in the water and on their way, the muffled roar of their engines disappearing into the night. Boats One and Two carried the assault mission's eight divers and shot off for a location two thousand meters off the entrance to the harbor of Coffin's Nail Reef while the other boats prepared to take up positions around the base's perimeter.

Michael "Mickey" Flynn, operational commander and skipper of the Number One Boat led the group towards the northeast at a comfortable forty-seven knots, taking advantage of the overcast skies. He knew that as the late evening wore on, a small squall was expected from the west, giving his team the additional coverage of rain.

A seasoned veteran of Tactical Extractions, Flynn was slightly apprehensive about leading an assault on a Chinese naval base. The base itself not providing the uneasiness as much as the modern nuclear sub that was supposed to be the primary target. This action was something wholly new to his resume of covert operations.

To set his mind at ease, he kept reminding himself of the fifty-five men that had worked on the ill-fated *Orient Task*. If the Chinese were involved – even remotely involved – in the sinking, then he had no reservations about taking out one of their biggest and best subs. This was the simple objective. The more difficult and hence more dangerous goal was to recover evidence that the Chinese possessed *Shkval* torpedoes.

Mickey Flynn knew intimately that the probability of finding torpedoes *off* the submarine was highly unlikely, necessitating the action of physically boarding the submarine. Something that didn't sit too well with him, even if the dive teams were more optimistic.

At a distance of about five nautical miles from the base, the six boats split up according to a pre-determined plan and sped off into the night. Only the two *Sea Tigers* that carried the divers remained within a short distance of each other as the two teams had to work in unison for the mission to succeed.

With the 20mm kinetic gun upfront, Flynn was confident that they could obliterate anything that they would come into contact with, short of a blue-water vessel such as a destroyer or cruiser. Having divers in the water, however, would place eight *individuals* directly in harm's way. This is what concerned him the most.

To respond to the possibility of diver detection, Flynn had developed a plan in which all six boats would fire their weapons into the base from their respective locations. By heading each craft directly at the heart of the island and firing the guns, their machine guns, and launching small rockets, it was hoped that there would be enough confusion for the divers to make a break for it.

Every man taking part in the mission – indeed including every man back on the *Arafura Sea Paradise* – expected to participate in some form of retribution for the loss of their comrades and, without exception, ignored the possibility that they may not make it back alive.

This solitary purpose kept the men focused as their small boats raced across the seas to rendezvous with a tiny rock that even the Chinese declared to be non-existent but which at the present harbored one of their most destructive naval vessels.

JASON LOOKED OVER the satellite images one last time. He possessed three views of a Chinese submarine nearing Coffin's Nail Reef, but none that expressly showed the vessel docking at the base. By the time the *SkyAction* satellite was back into prime position, the mission that he ordered against the Chinese base would be over.

More so than Sudan, this operation was taking a great deal of his attention away from other activities, namely his business interests. He was aggravated by the lack of a real-time aerial reconnaissance capability, something that had been suggested from the African operation and desperately wanted to develop key technologies that would permit such luxuries.

One luxury that he did have, however, was the knowledge that, unlike Sudan, the assault against the Chinese base was in direct response to the loss of the *Orient Task*. The world might've not cared about innocent babies as much as Jason Task, but he'd be damned if he was going to allow justice for the destruction of a ship and crew of his own be swayed by public opinion.

If there was one thing that the world knew about Jason Task, it was that he took matters into his own hands, particularly when his people or his businesses were threatened. This situation, was hardly any different, even if his adversary was an extremely large and populous nation such as China.

Regardless, Jason knew that he had one ally on his side; the Chinese couldn't acknowledge that they had anything to do with the sinking of the LNG carrier. If Beijing made any public response regarding the mission currently underway in the Spratly Island's, then all Jason simply had to do was present evidence of the *Shkval* torpedo that was found among the wreckage.

Of course, the Chinese didn't have any clue that Jason had in fact recovered the remains of the torpedo, but they would be hard pressed to prove that he had anything to do with the raid against an island that *they swore didn't exist either*. This is where Jason had the Beijing government's ass in a sling and he was going to maximize his effort against it.

There *would* be hell to pay, and he knew it. Even in clandestine warfare where the opposing parties never publicly admitted their involvement, each side continued to conduct operations against their opponent under the cloak of secrecy. Even if China remained quiet in the public eye, he knew they would be gunning for him and his businesses, something they could very well succeed in destroying.

Despite these risks, Jason was pressed hard against the wall; he had to punish those who attacked his ship. If he failed, or even hesitated to act, then his adversaries may conclude that he was either impotent or unwilling to protect his assets. By a quick, vicious, and justified response, Jason would inform the world's leaders that his operations were *not* to be tampered with.

Tactical Extractions tiptoed along the line, but his new Gatestrian Knights would charge along the path regardless of which way things fell. They wouldn't just merely move into an area, they would always be there, ready to strike a blow for justice and humanity. Whether or not the Knights would evolve into the organization that he envisioned depended very much on whether his Spratly Islands operation succeeded.

His confidence was lifted as he looked over the photographs that showed the speck of dried coral that constituted the bulk of the base. They could eliminate the island without effort had their primary target not been the nuclear submarine that he hoped was now tied to the pier and for which he overrode the operational commanders by ordering its destruction.

THE DARK SUITED divers slowly made their way into the harbor, the only indication of their presence being the miniscule luminosity of their compass dials. Using oxygen rebreathers and electric propulsion units, the commando teams effortlessly made their way into the inky blackness of the early morning sea.

Fred Price led Team One, consisting of four divers – himself, Alfred Freeman, Gene Fogas, and Chuck Gibson – who would force their way into the *Zhan shi*. Team Two, led by Harry Mattox and consisting of Gus Robertson, Kevin Rabun, and Al Hoover would provide security around the pier, protecting the team that attacked the submarine.

The two assault boats that delivered the divers remained a few thousand meters off the entrance to the harbor, floating idly in case they were needed to rush in to provide whatever assistance they could to the divers.

Detection, however, was not part of the dive team's objective and they had several contingency plans to thwart such discovery, particularly through launching a massive initial strike which would paralyze the rationalization process of all present on the sleepy, remote outpost.

After two hours of swimming, Fred Price's eyes detected a faint glow ahead that slowly increased in intensity until they silhouetted a cylindrical shape resting in the distance. His experience immediately recognized the teardrop hull of a modern submarine and adjusted his path to bring him and his team towards the stern of the submarine which had been positioned closest to the divers.

Soon, the portable lights that lined the pier provided enough visibility underwater for the assault team to observe each other and Price immediately motioned for his team to take advantage of the cover provided by the pier itself. The last thing that he wanted was for them to be spotted by some low-level dock worker relieving himself into the ocean below.

The four divers of Team One hid amongst the slime covered pilings, unable to keep their bodies from bobbing in the rain splattered surf due to the slippery organisms that made it nearly impossible to grip anything.

Time was not a luxury, and Price immediately motioned for Fogas and Gibson to set the main charge against the submarine's propeller. He and Alfred Freeman then swam underneath the hull of the submarine, barely squeezing beneath its hulk and the harbor floor, to reach the intake for the reactor's cooling pump.

Unconfirmed intelligence reports had the *Zhan shi* in for a cooling pump problem. This meant that not only would the reactor be shut down, but that with the pumped removed for repairs and/or replacement, there would be one less obstacle in the way of explosive output.

After a few moments of searching for the inlet, Price and Freeman found the elusive opening and quickly set about placing the explosives package into the orifice before returning towards the relative safety of the pier.

Gene Fogas and Chuck Gibson had an easier time placing their charge against the shaft seal just forward of the seven-bladed propeller, but had to move more quickly to avoid detection from those positioned on the pier. Their luck rested with the Chinese, who never seemed to be concerned about hostile swimmers within this remote outpost, and for the most part, dared not venture out into the pouring rain.

Harry Mattox and Kevin Rabun of Team Two bobbed at the surface next to one of the pilings, desperately trying to avoid making any noises or unnatural disturbances in the water. The slippery greenish slime prevented them from hugging the pile and instead had to straddle a length of misused rope that hung down beneath the pier and into the water.

In the distance, Mattox and Rabun could just make out the shapes of Gus Robertson and Al Hoover patrolling the far end of the pier, next to where the structure merged into the concrete foundation of the island itself. To their right, they observed the emergence of Team One as they swam towards the rickety, wooden gangplank that bridged the gap between the pier and the submarine.

Mattox looked at this watch. Five minutes before the charges were to go off. An eternity when one was trying to remain quiet deep in the midst of hostile territory. To their benefit was the muffled din of the submarine's emergency diesel generator which manifested itself with a bluish cloud emanating from the rear of the hull.

As he looked around his environment, aided by the pier lights, Mattox wondered how Price and the others were expected to make their way into the bowels of the submarine, the feat seemingly impossible from his vantage point.

His pondering of the situation was short-lived, however, for *his* mission was to protect those going aboard the submarine. This meant that he had to cover not only the sub itself but anyone who was or would be coming to the pier. The latter was the primary concern of Robertson and Hoover who were not only positioned at the beginning of the pier, but were setting their own charges that would blast a gap into the structure, preventing reinforcements – such as they were – from arriving from the shore.

At precisely the planned time, a column of water erupted from the stern of the submarine, catching everyone present by surprise as the mass of liquid showered down upon the vessel and the adjacent pier, casting numerous tiny rainbows as the droplets hung within the light. Lost within the confusion generated by the more noticeable stern explosion was the muffled roar and bubbling of the sea from the cooling inlet charge.

Fred Price immediately raised his silenced MP5 submachine gun above the water and fired several 9mm rounds into the guards that stood next to the gangplank, sending the dazed soldiers into a pirouetted dive into the water below.

Alfred Freeman followed his team leader up onto the gangplank, ignoring the powerful explosion that seemed to rip the far end of the pier into countless splinters, and headed directly towards the hatch opening within the vessel's conning tower.

Price grabbed the first individual exiting the hatch and threw the hapless sailor into the water below. With Freeman as his backup, he fired his weapon into the opening, then followed up the invasion with a hand grenade, ducking behind the open steel hatch to shield his body from the flying shrapnel.

Seconds later, he and Freeman stormed through the opening, laying a deadly band of bullets that ricocheted around in front of them before moving towards the bow of the submarine. Stunned Chinese sailors dropped to the deck, some dripping profusely with blood.

In less than a minute, the two commandos entered into the forward torpedo compartment, barely reaching the hatch before the submarine's crew tried in vain to seal off the section. Not wishing to blast away indiscriminately in a compartment loaded with volatile weapons, Price resorted to using his weapon as a baton, smashing it against the cranium of those standing in his way.

Freeman, for his part, retrieved a waterproof Sony camcorder from his backpack and immediately began videotaping the compartment, making certain that the vessel's torpedoes filled his camera's field of view. Of the six torpedoes that he witnessed, he knew that at least one seemed to be different, but he didn't have time to examine it in detail; their mission was to get into the compartment, videotape the surroundings, place a small charge near the torpedo rack, and vacate the premises as quickly as possible.

Fred Price set the delay on an explosives satchel, dropped it among a group of four torpedoes, then motioned for Freeman to follow him out of the compartment. Seeing a pair of sailors in front of him, Price leveled them with a blast from his MP5, then hurried over their bodies towards the still open hatch leading outside. The total time that he and Freeman spent inside of the vessel was less than two and a half minutes.

Bursting out into the open, both Price and Freeman hopped over the gangplank and dropped into the water below. Protecting their comrades' exit, Harry Mattox fired a volley from his MP5 into the direction of the submarine's conning tower, sending those out on deck diving into various directions. He then tossed a grenade onto the gangplank which exploded, shredding a large portion of the wooden brow.

Breaking radio silence, Gus Robertson radioed for the boats to execute an extraction under red – or combat – condition, before he and Hoover began a backwards swim towards the others.

18

WHEN THE CHARGE situated within the forward torpedo room detonated, it tore through the compartment with such force as to initiate secondary explosions within the weapons themselves. These rapid explosions lifted the submarine's bow up for several seconds before mercifully allowing the dying vessel to drop back down hard onto the floor of the harbor.

The mushrooming fireball from the final explosion bathed the entire island in an eerie orange-white glow that seemed to hang in the air for several minutes, and permitted Harry Mattox and Kevin Rabun to exit the water and head up into the shore facilities to search for further evidence.

This action had not been planned as a mission imperative objective, but was the result of a last minute, on the spot decision to search for clues as well as the whereabouts of the oft-reported but unconfirmed survivors of the *Orient Task*.

The arrival of Boat One and its partner provided an air of security as they used their 20mm kinetic guns to saw off the antennas of the rapidly sinking submarine as well as those that peppered the shore facilities, effectively eliminating the ability of the Chinese to call for assistance.

For the moment, the assault team held the island; the Chinese shore personnel were virtually not existent, many of whom had hid in storage facilities far from the battle scene and the sailors from the *Zhan shi* were distracted between saving their ship and saving their lives.

Mattox and Rabun cautiously entered the first building, sweeping its corridors clear with their MP5s at the ready, visually inspecting every room, and videotaping anything that seemed worth remembering.

The facility, despite being fairly new, was in a state of disrepair with holes and cracks within the walls and tile missing from the floors. It reminded Mattox more of a military prison than a support facility, and when they entered the fifth and final room, he realized how close his intuition was to the truth.

Thin, barely clothed, and tied to a small cot was a disheveled figure trying desperately to catch their attention. A sailor that both commandos recognized as one of the crewmembers of the ill-fated *Orient Task* from the pre-mission briefing photographs they were shown, but could not identify as of yet.

"Are you from the *Orient Task*?" questioned Mattox, raising his voice so that he could be heard through his breathing mask.

"Yes, yes." replied the barely audible individual, shaking slightly. "I am José Peña."

While Rabun set about cutting the ropes that bound the unfortunate sailor to the cot, Maddox held his microphone mouthpiece closer to his lips.

"This is Bravo Two Delta." Mattox spoke as he picked up the now freed Peña in a fireman's carry. "We have a package, repeat, we have a package."

"Roger, Bravo Two Delta." Fred Price's voice came over the radio earpiece, acknowledging their confirmation of a survivor from the wreck. "This is Bravo One Delta, we understand that you have a package and we will assist in the delivery. The vans are out front."

With Peña balanced over his left shoulder, Mattox motioned for Rabun to escort them out of the facility. "Let's get out of here!"

The two commandos plus prisoner exited the shabby building into a complete war zone with projectiles flying in from all points of the compass as the *Sea Tigers* took up positions all around the island. The sole return fire coming from a few sailors pinned down in the submarine's conning tower.

Fred Price and Alfred Freeman waited by the water's edge, signaling their location to the trio via flashlight while the other four divers made an earnest attempt to take out anything that moved.

Sea Tiger Boat Number One moved in towards the pier, using the light from the various explosions to illuminate their path through the shoals while Boat Number Two fired its rockets into the shore facility, distracting those on board the submarine who thought that the rockets would soon be targeted on them.

With an exceptional feat of seamanship, Mickey Flynn backed his boat up to the pier while crewmembers Danny Watson and Brad Scheer hauled down the weak but grateful Peña. Shortly afterward, all eight divers were brought aboard the single boat and Flynn launched a bright green flare that blossomed into the sky informing the five other boats that they were now fully loaded and heading back out towards the open sea.

With the various fires dying down, Flynn lost his optimal view of the shoal, but placed trust in his memory and roared out of the harbor at full throttle, the second boat, commanded by Chip Taylor, reeling around and covering his partner's rear.

JASON WALKED BRISKLY along the starboard deck of the *Sanctity* with Roberto Hernandez a short step behind. "You've confirmed that it is Third Officer Peña from the *Orient Task?*"

"Yes." Roberto nodded. "Weak, dehydrated, but in fair condition nevertheless."

"What about the *Zhan shi?*"

"The submarine was effectively sunk."

"Torpedoes?"

"We believe that it had two *Shkval*-type torpedoes on board."

"What about video?"

"We're waiting on a link right now. As you can probably understand, Mr. Task, our men are in the process of trying to get out of harm's way at the moment."

Jason paused, turning towards the western horizon which still remained dark even though the sun had appeared in the east. "Yes, of course. We need to get those men out of there."

"Yes, sir. The *Arafura Sea Paradise* will head towards Point Eleven Two Echo once the boats are retrieved."

"*Towards* China?"

Roberto shrugged his shoulders. "Captain Davis believes that nobody would suspect that the attackers would turn towards hostile territory. This might give them a chance to escape."

"I don't know." exhaled Jason as he spun around to retrace his steps back towards the main salon. "I'd just as soon send a fleet in there to escort them out. I mean, my God, Roberto, we just sunk a nuclear submarine!"

"A nuclear submarine that sunk *your* ship." reminded Roberto, now walking in step with his boss. "They made the first move."

"Do we have physical proof though?"

"From the description that was radioed in regarding Pena's testimony, it could've only been the Russians or Chinese and the Russians weren't anywhere near the region at the time of the sinking."

"Is that all they said? That he saw a blinding blue flash before the ship blew up? Nothing more?"

"That's all, sir. May I continue to remind you that they're only now getting back from the mission and once everyone's safe and Peña has been checked out by the medical staff we will get more answers."

"Yeah, I know, but I need answers and lots of them. Before long, China is going to be hunting us down like rabbits and I want everyone within our organization to retreat behind our safety lines before they figure out who hit the *Zhan shi*."

Jason stepped into the main salon, leaving Roberto to continue on to his cabin, and logged into his laptop which sat on the large table. He wanted to examine the preliminary post-action report that would be posted once the attack boats were recovered by the *Arafura Sea Paradise*, an event that he expected to take place within the hour.

He had long since ordered the *Sanctity* to head towards Guam, taking an indirect route through Micronesia to throw off anyone tracking her path. The yacht's helicopter had previously departed for Brunei where it would ultimately intercept the *Arafura Sea Paradise* and transport José Peña to better medical facilities.

Frustrated by the wait for news from the South China Sea, Jason decided to tinker with his plans for the Gatestrian Knights. His entire empire was now on a war footing, knowing that for whatever the reason that the Chinese sank his gas tanker, it was merely the start of hostilities against his organizations and his swift response would only heighten the conflict.

He now concluded that the Gatestrian Knights would offer two distinct organizations. The first would be a clandestine group of people who would mingle with society and basically serve as 'Gentlemen Knights' who would ensure that people are protected from harm, that class and culture would prevail and that the normally inattentiveness of the general public would not interfere with the evolution of civilization and moral standards.

These Gentlemen Knights, or GK's, would wear business suits, pack side arms for protection, and be as chivalrous as the medieval knights were. In short, the GK's would lead by example; they would wear suits and hats everywhere, even when the general populace rarely dressed for Sunday Mass, hold doors open for all women, and viciously attack criminals whenever they encountered them.

The second organization, which he christened the Sea Berets, would be an all-around military force, capable of launching strikes against tyrannical military forces anywhere in the world. The Sea Berets would be as deadly as the GK's were cultured.

This combination of chivalrous example and tactical enforcement was, in his opinion, what the world most desperately needed at the moment. A civilian force guided by moral principle and backed by military strength would go a long way towards eliminating both political ineptitude and radical destruction.

The biggest challenge was how to create an effective organization quickly without jeopardizing the entire process by sacrificing quality or integrity. Another problem afforded by necessity was that the

Gatestrian Knights would not be paid as well as his Tactical Extractions employees; Jason wanted a large organization but one where its members weren't motivated by financial expectations.

The Gatestrian Knights were to be idealists, motivated by a keen desire to serve the world, to help the defenseless, to chastise those in power or influence who diluted the concept of evil, and to defeat such evil whenever they came into contact with it.

Yet, there was more to his ambitions than merely combating evil as he saw it, Jason wanted to create a new civilization. He wanted to unify the world while maintaining its diversity and cultural treasures. For humanity to truly evolve, he realized, it must become a space-based civilization, shedding the umbilical with its native home.

A slight, pulsing tone brought Jason's thoughts back down to earth as he realized that the transmission of the post-action report came in several minutes earlier. He was most interested in the video of the sole surviving crewmember of the ill-fated *Orient Task*, the solitary witness to the catastrophe.

"Please state your name and position." spoke the authoritative voice originating from somewhere behind camera's view.

"José Peña, Third Officer of the *Orient Task*." The third mate sat in front of the camera seated at a small table, dressed smartly in blue coveralls.

"Please explain the events surrounding your vessel's disappearance."

Peña twitched in his seat, trying to remember all of the details of the disaster. "I was on the bridge during the midnight to six watch. The weather was clear, minimal seas."

"Were there other vessels present?"

"I could not see any vessels. There was a small blip on the radar to our stern, but I could not make visual contact."

"What was the last thing that you remember from being on the ship?" the voice of the invisible interviewer asked, seeming to prod a reluctant memory.

"I was on the port wing of the bridge." continued Peña, slightly more apprehensive about the subject. He wasn't exactly sure he was speaking with people friendly to him. After all, he had been whisked from a Chinese naval base in the middle of the night and though the commandos spoke English and *said* they were Americans, he couldn't be certain.

"Please continue." insisted the voice.

"It's... it's hard. I saw a small flash just forward of the superstructure along the waterline, near Tank Five. It was a bluish flash, almost like lightning but wider and more transparent.

"I leaned over the railing to see what it was. The next thing that I remember, I was floating in the water. It was horrible! There was fire all around! I couldn't find the ship! It was nowhere!"

Jason watched an arm dressed in a blue, long sleeved shirt reach in front of the camera and set a glass of water on the table in front of the sailor.

"Thank you." Peña replied, muffling his voice with a long drink from the glass, cleared his throat, and then continued. "I don't remember how long I was in the water. I found something that was floating and I pulled myself up on it."

"How did you get to the Chinese base?" questioned the interviewer.

"I don't remember. I kept blacking out, seeing strange people looking down at me. I couldn't move, like I was strapped to the bed or something.

"At first I thought that I was on a ship. Then I remembered seeing walls of a building. That's all that I remember until I was rescued from the island."

"Do you know anything about the submarine that was at the island?"

Peña shook his head softly, reflecting upon his internment at the base. "I'm sorry, I couldn't understand much of what was said." after a few more moments of reflection, a thought brightened his facial expressions as well as his posture. "I remember hearing a voice tell me that it was lucky that the submarine found me alive."

"Oh?"

"Yes. I think that maybe that's why I thought that I was on a ship. I don't remember them picking me up. I don't remember being taken off of the vessel. I just have glimpses of different times."

"Would you please tell us of your treatment at the naval base?"

Peña's posture fell; he leaned forward heavily upon the table. "I only remember being tied up. I couldn't move. I wasn't fed or allowed to use the lavatory. I wasn't in pain, I was just constrained."

The video paused on this final frame as Jason reached up and turned off the computer. It was obvious to him that Peña was under duress during his stay on the island. Whether by stress or perhaps by some form of medication, the sailor was unaware of the timeline of his stay at the base.

The mentioning of the bluish flash just before the ship sunk was highly indicative of some form of electromagnetic weapon, but in and of itself was not definitive proof that the disaster was caused by just such a device or that the Chinese could even be involved in the sinking.

"WELL, THEY'RE DEFINITELY *Shkval* torpedoes." spoke Dr. Clarence Brier whose face appeared on the videophone. "Maybe not originals, but darn good copies."

Dr. Bogdan Gritsenko's image appeared in the distance, behind his associate's left shoulder. "I concur."

"That's a definite confirmation?" questioned Jason, shaving himself in the bathroom, only slightly concerned about the images that appeared on the computer monitor.

"Yes." replied Brier, wondering why his employer had disappeared from his view. "Sir, are you still there?"

"I'm here in the head, trying to get a shave in. Tell me what you can about the warheads on the torpedoes."

"That's somewhat difficult. As you may know, the forward section of a *Shkval* torpedo consists of the gas discharge system. The warhead's basically buried in the torpedo itself."

"So there's no way of knowing what kind of warhead was on the torpedoes?" Jason walked out into the salon, still completing his shave, in order to allow his engineers a chance to view the one whom they were corresponding with.

"Not from the video." replied Brier. "You would have to look at the real thing."

Jason nodded. The last thing that he wanted to do was send in another team to retrieve the evidence, knowing full well that the Chinese were probably planning a salvage effort at the very moment.

"Could we get a satellite image during the recovery process that would enable us to determine the type of warhead?" Jason asked, returning to the bathroom to complete his shave before splashing a handful of water onto his face to rinse off the shaving cream.

Brier frowned. "The satellite would have to be in the right place at exactly the right time and under the best possible of conditions."

"In other words." Jason grumbled. "We can't make any determinations unless we're on-site. How close are we to having an aerial recon capability?"

"A few weeks at best. Not good enough to help with the current situation, I'm afraid."

"Well, I'm going to order a dedication of our satellite assets, just to do what we can do. Would it be possible to develop an autonomous vehicle that could survey the harbor while the salvage operation is underway?

"I do not believe so." Clarence Brier turned to confer with his colleague, then continued. "We believe that any system large enough to provide adequate images would be detected immediately. I'm afraid there's no way to get concrete, physical evidence without someone being there."

"Thank you, Doctors." Jason turned off his computer and folded it before heading into the bathroom to shower.

What his engineers had told him basically was that he needed human intelligence more than electronic or photographic intelligence. While this was decidedly not impossible, it was very difficult owing to the restrictive nature of the Chinese government. Either by bribe or by emplacement, obtaining on-site intelligence from a human person was an exceptionally troublesome method of operation, often requiring years of planning and support – things that couldn't be done on the spot.

Without this information, however, he was pitted against a major nation who – if they so chose to admit their presence in the area – could simply deny their involvement in the *Orient Task* affair, thereby implicating Jason Task in the destruction of a multimillion dollar piece of naval hardware and the death of several crewmembers.

Coming on the heels of the Sudanese operation, Jason feared that world opinion would rear up against him, never minding the fact that both raids were initiated in response to the death of dozens of innocent people – children in the case of Africa and sailors in the present instance.

He needed hard facts, *physical* proof that the rocket torpedo found within the wreckage was fired by the Chinese submarine that his forces sank at Coffin's Nail Reef. He knew that he simply could present the remains of the weapon, state that it was Chinese and appeared within the debris field, and let everyone decide for themselves.

The problem was – and this fact necessitated the need for the Gatestrian Knights – there was always someone who looked at the evidence, listened to the facts, and still cast their vote against common sense. These individuals were the ones who Jason scolded as believing in alien visitations, faked lunar landings, and who elevated entertainers to the ranks of deities.

Believing that his only course of action was to hold firm to his methods, Jason concluded that the burden of proof was on the Chinese. Who, after all, would believe that a simple businessman could orchestrate such a raid against the powerful Chinese navy? This *wasn't* Sudan.

Jason knew deep down that it was a weak argument at best; his businesses had pulled off some of the most technological triumphs of the past several decades. His aerospace company's Europa probe, for one, discovered the organic sludge that drifted between the Jovian moon's liquid oceans and the ice shelves that dominated the satellite.

Such feats were, quite literally, astronomically difficult in comparison with the mere sinking of a broken down submarine stuck at a remote outpost. Jason knew that even those senseless individuals that he so despised would be inclined to believe that he had not only the technology but the finances and people necessary to pull off the feat.

His only recourse, therefore, was to prepare for both a public and private battle against the Chinese government where the stakes were basically the survival of each participant. This war would require both defensive and offensive capabilities, signaling a long-term commitment on his part.

One thought, however, tore at Jason's mind. *What was the true reason for the Chinese attack on his ship?* He had many theories, but no real motives with which to go by. He wondered whether further assets were being targeted, even before his assault on Coffin's Nail Reef.

19

JACK STEPHENS LED his guest onto the patio, walking past the towering stone waterfall that flowed through the lush tropical landscaping into the sparkling pool of his expansive Palm Bay residence. The brilliant afternoon sunshine beamed through the glass, creating a warm and humid atmosphere within the large enclosure.

"You can see our problem." replied the visitor as he occupied a white wicker chair next to a circular glass table. "President Decatur *must* stop Mr. Task from carrying out his private wars; the actions of your friend are placing the position of the United States in serious jeopardy."

Jack calmly selected a chair next to his guest, after nonchalantly adjusting the multicolored umbrella that provided shade for the pair. "I'm not aware that Jason is involved in any wars, Mr. Butler."

"Please, Mr. Stephens." Terrence Butler didn't accept Jack's lie. "Your friend has already overthrown one nation, and his fingerprints are all over another event that recently happened in the South China Sea region."

Jack retained his composure, not wishing to implicate his friend if the feds didn't really have anything on him. "Are you referring to that situation in Sudan where General Kuraymahiyyun was overthrown by the locals?"

Butler still maintained his diplomatic stance, but frustration occasionally flashed within his eyes. "Mr. Stephens, we are fully aware that you supported *his* actions in Khartoum, and is it not your foundation that is, as we speak, providing food and medical supplies?"

"It's my wife's foundation, yes."

"Is what's your wife's not also yours?"

Jack never did like politicians. "So you've come all the way here to inform me to stop sending food and medicine into Sudan. That wouldn't be very popular."

"Actually, Mr. Stephens, I'm here regarding Mrs. Stephens."

Jack tensed up. "Jamie? She's in Europe; what does she have to do with this?"

"President Decatur is very impressed with your wife's credentials. He would very much like to nominate her as ambassador to the Vatican."

"Ambassador?" Jack was now completely in defensive mode, not believing that all of this concerned his wife. "Jamie?"

"Yes, Mr. Stephens. The President feels that she would be ideal for the position. She's articulate, educated, generous with her wealth and multi-lingual so she could communicate with the diverse population associated with the Holy See."

"And you came all the way here to speak with me when my wife is in Vienna?"

"Yes, Mr. Stephens. The President is very concerned about *your* activities. He's afraid that these kinds of operations would severely jeopardize Mrs. Stephens' chances to be confirmed."

Jack never liked dabbling in politics, but he fully understood the principle of *quid pro quo*. "Tell me, Mr. Butler, has the President contacted my wife regarding this position?"

Terrence Butler remained silent for a few moments, feigning interest in the waterfall that flowed into the peanut-shaped pool. "We thought it best to confer with you first."

"In other words, Terry." Jack, having finally penetrated through the smoke screen, decided that it was time to forego the diplomatic pretense. "I stop my involvement with Jason and the President will *reward* me by nominating my wife as Ambassador to the Vatican."

"I wouldn't say reward *you*; your wife has truly earned the position."

"Jamie's earn the role of president in my book."

Terrence Butler nervously shifted in his seat. "Of course she has. Yet, could she accomplish that goal with your involvement with Jason Task? After all, the media would devour her background for anything that would be considered unethical."

Jack did all he could to refrain from knocking out his visitor right then and there. "This is extortion."

"Extortion, Jack? You've been implicated as an accomplice of Jason Task who's known to have taken place in several international incidents that, at best, are truly horrendous. I think that the President's been most generous. Is not your wife more important than your friend?"

Jack's emotions tipped the scale from merely being frustrated to being pissed off as hell. Whereas many husbands simply loved their wives, Jack idolized Jamie. She was not just part of his life, she was his *whole* life, so much so that when Jason lost Samantha, Jack spent months smothering Jamie with attention – something that didn't quite dissipate with time.

He didn't even know if Jamie wanted to become an ambassador, but knew that she wanted to give something more to the community than just contributions or jobs. She wanted to give back *time* to the country that had served her so well.

Had it been any other country, Jack wouldn't question it, but he knew deep down that Jamie wouldn't pass this chance being the devout Catholic that she was. What Terrence Butler offered was an excellent way of targeting both him and Jason Task, using Jamie as the projectile.

Jack stood up, anchoring his hands firmly to the table. "Tell Decatur that I'll do what is right."

HAL JORDAN STOOD in front of the group, admiring them with a certain sense of pride that he kept tucked neatly inside of his thoughts. "You gentlemen are the first of a special organization.

"You were selected because you combine the integrity, honesty, strength, intelligence, and, for lack of better words, the anonymity required to carry out your mission.

"You will be the ones who stand idly by until life is threaten. You will then do whatever you can to provide assistance. You are chivalrous beyond compare; you are kind, considerate, but above all protective. You are the Secret Service for the common man."

Jordan walked among the group handing out bound documents, a half inch thick each. "This is your contract, your code of conduct if you will. It is thick, yes, but so is the cloak of common sense.

"In this world, there are many who subscribe to the culture of death. They promote abortions on demand, euthanasia, free sex, and a host of other social ills. Someone has to devote their life to ridding the world of these abominations. *You* are that someone.

"During the course of the future, you will be joined by hundreds of others who share these values. In time, thousands will join you as we graduate new adults into the world from our schools. Every one of them will share your belief in creating a greater civilization, one that respects women and children, abhors crime, and most of all, believes that God is the One who truly rules."

Jordan finished handing out the documents and returned to the front of the room. "People, I must emphasize that you are *not* vigilantes. You will not break the law; you will not create your own laws. What you will do, however, is maximize the potential inherent within the law.

"If your state, for example, permits carrying firearms, you will carry such. Not for the destruction of life. On the contrary, for the preservation of life – *innocent* life!"

"Can you clarify our mission any?" spoke one of the attendants, seated within the front row.

"Yes, Eddie." replied Jordan, exercising the patience learned from his years as a university professor. "Gentlemen, let me explain your function, this way.

"Have you ever been at Mass, and heard people desecrate the sanctity of the environment by speaking loudly of such things as their hernia operation? Perhaps you've witnessed occasions where the priest changed the liturgy or openly supported teachings in direct conflict with Church law?

Maybe you had witnessed a mugging when no one else was around to provide assistance, or knew of someone who was laid off and had a spouse or child that needed medical attention and couldn't afford it?

These are all examples of where a single individual, making an effort to influence change can make all the difference in the world."

Jordan walked over to where Eddie Cummings sat. "Eddie, the world doesn't always need a cowboy personality armed with a six-shooter. Sometimes, all that's required is the gift of the pen, and a sound editorial regarding the sad state of affairs within the world."

"What happens when literary talent fails?" questioned Todd Sims somewhat sarcastically from across the room.

Hal Jordan walked in his direction, but did not look at Sims directly, preferring to address everyone. "If someone pulls a gun on you, shoot the bastard.

"Gentlemen, I won't whitewash your function by not saying that you will be judge, jury, and executioner. Your role with be that and much more. What sets you apart, however, from the thugs, villains, and morons that pretend to offer a better way of life is that you will be accountable to the highest moral standards.

"You will act with perfection; when laws break down, you will shore then up. When politicians and social authorities try to dilute moral standards, you will hold them accountable. And, most importantly, when innocent lives come into danger, you will respond like a grizzly bear defending his den."

"All of us are veterans of Tactical Extractions." spoke Rodney Baker, shifting his wire rimmed eyeglasses, trying desperately to avoid creating trouble. "Most of us, I am certain, have already pledge ourselves to these ideals. What *I* want to know, and I am sure everybody else has this on their mind, is what is it that makes the Gatestrian Knights so special?"

Confirmation in the form of quiet rumblings filled the room. Hal Jordan permitted the whispers to continue for a period, before re-establishing his authority.

"Gentlemen." Jordan continued. "Jason Task wants to create a new civilization, one that can take humanity into outer space, perhaps. What happens several hundred years in the future is not of my concern, at the moment.

"However, each one of us has seen the decline of Western civilization, religion, and morality. Humanity is doomed to fail if we do not get off of this planet and we're not going anywhere if we allow ourselves to drift back into the Dark Ages.

"As you will read in your documentation, the Gatestrian Knights will *civilize* society; the Sea Berets will defend it. Both the United States and the United Nations, as well as their various underpinnings, are hamstrung by politics. We won't be.

"People, we've all seen Hollywood westerns where the hero takes matters into their own hands, shoots up the bad guys, screws the woman who looks as though she hasn't gone a day without make-up, and rarely, if ever, gets injured. That's fiction, people! This is reality.

"Nobody here must be thinking of glory. Not on *my* watch! You want to play hero, go join a foreign legion somewhere."

Jordan paused a few minutes, cooling his emotions, before continuing. "What Jason Task wants, I believe, is that each person becomes a mix of being a policeman, a medic, a priest, and a victim's advocate.

"By the time an individual could become an *ideal* Knight, he would have become a weapons expert, proficient in multiple languages, possess multidisciplinary scientific and engineering knowledge, be devout in their faith, and develop an almost mythical martial arts capability. Forget what you hear about from the media or the movies; these characteristics must be the genuine thing. No exceptions."

JASON WALKED BRISKLY around the cabin of his Boeing 777, stretching his legs during the long flight from Guam to Oklahoma City following his rather unexpected conversation with Jack Stephens.

He was depressed, a little angry, and very concerned over his future plans. At the same time, however, he couldn't blame Jack; his friend and cousin wasn't the one turning the thumb screws. It was the politicians who sacrificed justice for the sake of diplomacy who had effectively bribed Stephens out of participation within the Gatestrian Knights project, and more importantly from his involvement with Tactical Extractions.

Had Jason been in the same position with Samantha being offered the ambassadorship, he probably would've made the same decision. Still, he firmly believed that Jamie Stephens had not been so honored because of her outstanding credentials; Washington didn't function on such realities.

Jamie Stephens had been offered the position because her husband was a confidant and partner of Jason who had already overthrown one despotic regime and had since destroyed a communist submarine which had – though quite circumstantially – destroyed a gas carrier.

Jason was incensed that he was being thwarted in his attempt to carry on the battle against evil. Whether in open combat or covert operation, politicians always had a way of screwing the pooch and the world ultimately suffered.

Just as the Gatestrian Knights were beginning to be organized, the world's most powerful politician had succumbed to the world's most persistent vice: money. Jason believed, truly believed, that the Chinese had found a way to sabotage his efforts without either admitting that they occupied Coffin's Nail Reef or possessed any *Shkval* torpedoes.

What really disturbed Jason, however, was the realization that, although he could admit his activities were significant, the whole affair appeared to be a case of 'sending the child to the bedroom without dinner' as Jack always called it. Jason called it appeasement of an enemy.

When he first committed himself to the plan, Jason was more of an idealist than a pessimist. This latest action darkened his motives, something that seemed to aggravate his plans for the future. Whereas before he wanted to provide something of a religious crusade, he now wanted to dominate the world's policies.

He possessed wealth – with Jack, he represented a twenty billion dollar chunk of American free enterprise – but he never devoted his entire empire to his goals. That had changed around the time that he sent commandos into Khartoum. Now, simply being a religious zealot was no longer sufficient. He had to redefine religion and redesign his very being.

Jason Task had always been restrained by that one thing that handicapped Western armies – it wasn't *Christian* to engage in open warfare or assassinate political leaders or do just about anything else that those on the other side did freely and without reservation.

No power, whether individual or national in composure could fight the bad guys while adhering to the laws of civilization. This is why terrorists performed so well; by simply being who they were they gained a certain level of authority whereas those who were fighting against them *had* to function under Western, civilized procedures otherwise the entire planet would decry foul.

Jason was frustrated to the point of numbness. What little feeling that he had after Samantha's death was rapidly fading as the world went about its business, irrespective of whether children in Sudan were being murdered or sailors in Asia were being blown to bits.

Nobody would do anything unless someone like him took up the cause, only to be thrust into the cauldron of *pawnism* – the unique way of conducting international diplomacy through scapegoats, independent agents, and rules set by political figures who rarely served more than a decade in power.

Jason's power was in the form of currencies, precious metals, natural resources, and consumer products. They were earned, acquired, created, and produced. They weren't manufactured by popular vote.

He paused in his strolls around the aircraft cabin, to view the copy of the U.S. Declaration of Independence that he proudly displayed on the aft bulkhead, next to the door that led into the master suite. Such vision, he believed, was exactly the kind of thing that the world needed most today.

Jason could not take on the entire planet directly, but he could apply his vast resources to selected pressure points that could influence those who tried to prevent his ambitions. Just as a single individual could be dropped by a powerful punch to a key organ, any nation could succumb just as easy to a properly applied strike.

Stop Saudi Arabia from exporting oil and it would collapse. Prevent China from exporting products to the world, and it would lose its influence. Boycott the United Nations, and the world would spiral into either imperialism or feudalism.

Jason had to find a way to strike at the *world's* pressure point, not just a few nation's weaknesses. If he was going to convince the planet to act together, and ultimately rise off of this world, then he had to grab their undivided attention. *How does one grab the attention of an entire planet?*

He thought about the question for several minutes before realizing the answer revolved around the impending destruction of the planet itself. The implications of even thinking about this subject forced him to take a chair and sit down. *The destruction of the planet?*

This was not a vague notion; it was based upon simple fact. Only when the world was embroiled within a truly global war were nations inclined to assist one another. Would it be any different than if there was a more significant threat against it?

After a few minutes of soul searching, Jason thought about threats to the world as a whole. Wars? The world was used to them by now. Diseases? If AIDS, influenza, and the common cold didn't scare anybody, the world was immune to the threat of the diseases if not the diseases themselves.

Jason leaned back in his chair, realizing that there weren't many things that really, truly concerned the planet as a whole. Then he had a most revealing thought: there weren't many things *on this planet* that scared the world as a whole.

No, the human species was far too familiar with this planet to be scared of most things. Events originating from *off* the planet, however, was a totally different story altogether. He thought about extraterrestrial threats, legitimate ones. The only threat that his mind could comprehend was the inevitable collision with a comet or an asteroid. If this were the case, how could one convince the world that it was threatened by a planetary body *unless such a body was on a direct collision course with the earth?*

Jason toyed with the thought, ignoring the West Coast landscape that appeared through the cabin windows. Even a small asteroid, if known to the world, would gather a great deal of attention if it were even to come close to the planet. Unfortunately, as he was well aware, such threats rarely came about – most being discovered only *after* they passed the Earth's orbit.

Then, somewhere high above California, an intriguing thought came to him. *Why did he have to wait for an asteroid to come close to the Earth?* He reached across the conference table and grabbed a steno book that laid in front of him, immediately setting about to perform some quick calculations in the tan notepad.

With the success of their Europa probes, Jason's aerospace company – Jaserospace – had significant experience in conducting operations between Mars and Jupiter, particularly with the rendezvous and analysis of small planetary bodies. If there were some way to adjust the orbit of a small planetary body such as an asteroid, it could be deflected in towards the Earth.

Save for the flight crew, Jason had been alone on the flight, but he felt nowhere near as alone as he did when he fully contemplated the thoughts that flowed through his fatigued mind. Was he actually considering the targeting of the Earth by an asteroid?

He stood back up to return to his pacing habit, an activity he felt would circulate more blood to his tired brain. There had to be another method. *Think!*

Jason decided that sending an asteroid on a collision course with the Earth would be criminal at best, and conflict with his natural tendency to protect innocent lives and not harm them. It would also be decidedly difficult, if only for ensuring that the body would scare and not terminate those present on the home planet.

One thought did, however, earn his further analysis. Perhaps it wasn't so critical that the planetary body be sent on an intersecting course with the Earth? Perhaps it was merely sufficient to show the *capability?* The thought processes were flowing more clearly now and Jason returned to his calculations at the table.

If he were to intercept an asteroid, say for the legitimate purpose of mining its billions of dollars worth of metals, would it be any further a leap of the imagination for the political and military elite on the planet to assume that he could direct the body on just such a collision course with little or no additional effort?

Jason concluded that such intimidation, for lack of a better description, would be enforced more efficiently if his company *actually moved* the target body to another location, thereby proving his ability to send such a body on a possible collision course with the Earth.

Cupping his hands behind his head, he considered the raw power inherit within an individual that could manipulate the very orbits of such massive bodies. A slight shove here, a tweak there, and he could have an entire planet trembling in their feet.

20

JASON STARED QUIETLY at the Oklahoma City skyline, contemplating his future actions in light of recent developments.

"It's both of our decisions." replied Jack, standing next to his friend, arms crossed. "It's the only way that Jamie can accept the ambassadorship with honor."

"But to sell me your companies? Even Jamie's?"

Jack smiled. "Wealth can be a hindrance for a diplomat, really. We decided that your mission is as important as will be Jamie's new role."

Jason shook his head calmly, trying to dissuade his friend from forfeiting a life's dream. "How can you walk away from your business, your desire to explore the oceans?"

"Listen, Jason. It's *Jamie's* decision. She wants you to continue your work, to have the additional resources that you need."

"The future Ambassador to the Vatican wants me to blow up the planet?" laughed Jason, not buying into the irony.

"No, of course not. She does, however, want you to work towards your more, shall I say, diplomatic goals. She can help by being at the Vatican."

"I don't know, Jack. I smell Decatur's influence all over this appointment. I can't guarantee that I won't charge off on some tangent and actually try to do some damage to this planet.

"If the President came up with this solution to eliminate your involvement, selling me your businesses wouldn't remove Jamie or you from media scrutiny."

"I agree." replied Jack. "But wouldn't it piss off Decatur?"

"I bet it would, but I don't think that you realize my mental state at the present. I'm frustrated, angry at the world, depressed over missing Samantha. You name it! I want to change the world, yes, but sometimes I get so damn angry that I want to literally rip it apart."

Jack remained silent; he knew that his friend was tormented over his plans.

Jason walked over to his leather chair and sat down, a slight hiss sounded from the air that escaped as he lowered his body into the seat. "Jack, you know that I'm ambitious if not eccentric. If I take over your businesses and, God forbid, go totally nuts with my plans, the world will target you and Jamie out for being the ones who allowed me to significantly increase my wealth and resources."

"Listen, Jace. I've been here for two hours now, hearing you outline your plans for the Gatestrian Knights. It's a sound idea. If you're afraid that you'll do something really bad, just place several members of the Knights on your board and stop acting as a dictator. Be *business-like* in your approaches to change the world.

"Remember, Jason. Slight adjustments, over time, can do as much as significant changes done quickly. Be forceful, yes, but use that Jason Task element of common sense that succeeded so well in Khartoum.

"Be quick when all indications show sloth. Be powerful when all indications show weakness. Be persuasive when all indications show ineptitude."

Jason smiled, spinning within his chair to face his friend. "A page straight out of Sun Tzu."

Jack shrugged his shoulders. "Hey, it works for Japanese automakers."

"I'd have more confidence without implicating you and Jamie." replied Jason. "I have nothing left in life. You, however, have a beautiful wife and your young son. Hell, that's what life's all about! Me? I'm just myself; I can't harm anyone merely by association."

"Well, it's your decision. Jamie and I have to reduce our holdings anyway. Who knows? Maybe the next buyer will be worse than you? Ever think about that?"

"I'd prefer not being the one who'd ruin what you've spent twenty years developing."

Jack smiled, heading towards the door. "It'll be quite some time before all of this comes to fruition. So just think about it. Who knows, maybe things will warrant a change in either of our plans.

"Listen, Jamie just wanted to offer you the chance to acquire our companies. After all, you *are* family, such as it is. As for me, I'll be living in Italy and there won't be much time for running a global operation.

"If I sell my company, I'll be able to do what I've always wanted to do – study marine archaeology within the Mediterranean Sea. Now, I've got to head over to Dallas for some business. Jason, I can't tell you what to do, but if you want to buy us out, we're giving you the option before we formally seek outside buyers."

JASON WALKED DOWN the street, losing himself in amongst the crowd. It was his habit to occasionally duck out and just go for a walk, free from business constraints, security escorts, and the rest of the trappings of a corporate executive. Regardless of his current situation, he always remembered that three-quarters of his life was spent in borderline poverty.

Unlike those who inherited money, Jason was firmly grounded to the hard-working, spend-thrifty environment of the masses that he alternately hid among or from. He longed for the old days, most especially because Samantha was with him to guide his activities.

Those days were gone, and he knew it. His life was empty and where Samantha had once figured prominently was a huge hole in his soul that had to be filled with some other project. Coming to the rescue was his Gatestrian Knights organization, but this was undeniably a long-term goal, one spanning decades if not centuries.

Passing block after block, Jason examined the people that he came across, wondering what unique gifts each offered. The beggar on the corner who was the recipient of a five dollar bill out of Jason's pocket. He could've been as wealthy as Jason himself, but nobody would've known for certain if not for his actions and appearance.

He came across another person holding a sign that read "JESUS SAVES!" but wondered whether the enthusiastic street evangelist could possibly have comprehended the sheer size and complexity of the universe. Was he just another individual who believed that God was some bearded old man sitting on a cloud?

Jason passed a pair of teenagers, one of which was chatting on a cell phone regarding their curfew at eleven o'clock, admitting that "My parents bought me this cell phone so they can reach me if I'm late."

He shook his head at the sight. *My God, some parent wasted money on a cellular phone so their kid could run around town at night?* Watching the teenagers disappear around a corner, Jason proceeded with his late afternoon stroll, absorbing the sights and sounds of the city.

Any one of the people that he walked past could've been in severe trouble at any moment. Would any of them possibly benefit from the Gatestrian Knights? If he was just another pedestrian, could he possibly know that, perhaps, a Knight walked among them?

Jason examined the faces of the people who shared the sidewalk, noted their mannerisms and idiosyncrasies, and imagined their backgrounds. Were the ones dressed smartly in suits businessmen, or job searchers? Were the women who wore loose fitting clothes mothers or cleaning ladies?

With such a diverse group to examine, Jason concluded that it was virtually impossible to adhere to any stereotypes. Of the thousands that he had come across, there were probably examples from every category.

One thought had occurred to him, however. Of the hundreds of people that he had examined in detail, none seemed to have noticed *him*. They walked past him, next to him, and even bumped into him. Yet, nobody actually observed him as intensely as he was looking at them!

Jason marveled at the thought – here he was a multibillionaire strolling down the street considering the salvation of the entire human species and not one person could afford the time to notice him. He chuckled to himself as he continued on his way.

Before long, he realized that he had ventured sixteen blocks from his office building, ending deep into the southwest corridor of the city. The city buildings had long since given way to strip malls, motels, and restaurants. Neither interested in spending money or eating, Jason decided to retrace his steps.

He did in fact learn a great deal from his excursion; he realized that people were too tied up in their daily lives to consider events on a truly global scale. People were, he remembered, largely interested in placing food on the table and keeping their kids out of trouble.

Morality, religion, and international events were things to be discussed within like-minded groups and not given much thought on a continual basis. All of this led credence to Jason's theory that *someone* had to intervene on their behalf. Someone who not only could identify threats against them, but someone who had the capability to defend them.

Was this the confirmation that he so desperately sought? Did these people really need him to act on their behalf? Jason's walk took on a more decisive, militaristic cadence as he headed back towards his office.

He knew now what he had to do; he had to work aggressively to develop the Gatestrian Knights into a true global operation. He also had to restructure Tactical Extractions into the Sea Berets – the military arm of the Knights. None of this was going to be easy, or even quick.

With no further doubt, the Gatestrian Knights were going to be his major project, the absorber of his precious time. Perhaps, however, he had erred in his initiation of action. No, he thought, those babies in Sudan needed to be avenged and, well, the Chinese needed to be punished.

The one thing that sat heavily on his soul was the true reason for the attack on his ship. Sure, the Chinese did it, but *why*? What did the

Beijing government expect to gain from launching a pre-emptive strike against a commercial ship?

He had read a brief intelligence report that somehow, some way, Beijing was involved with the militaristic government of General Kuraymahiyyun of Sudan. He didn't know the reason or even the implications if this were true, but knew that such international covert alliances were nothing unusual.

For the moment, he had to make his way back to the office. There, he would be able to collect his thoughts, as well as analyze all of his reports. The walk did allow him to make a few decisions that played on his consciousness. One, he would delve into the creation and organization of the Gatestrian Knights. Two, he would accept Jack and Jamie Stephens' offer to purchase their company, effectively doubling his operations, though more for appearance sake as Jack nearly always went along with his suggestions.

Debt service may slow down his progress, but the acquisition could only benefit his objective in the long run. By adding ocean engineering and pharmaceuticals directly into his empire, he would be able to greatly affect the global population and, perhaps, influence their choice in leaders and policies.

JASON DIDN'T NOTICE the silver Thunderbird jump the curve, the wayward automobile being something of a dark blotch that didn't register as anything particularly threatening.

When his mind had sufficient time to warn of danger, the actions transmitted to his limbs were no longer of use. The blinding blackness of impact was followed quickly by lightning bolts of confusion, pain, and the sensation of hurling through the air in a feat of weightlessness.

Amidst screams of women and of crunching metal, he had the distinct sensation of seeing people pass *underneath* him, but he could not be certain as the normally free flowing imagery of life seemed to stop and snapshots of daily life took their place, interspersed with shades of black.

He could not feel any pain, but he could not register feeling within his limbs either. His eyes observed swirling motions of people and scenes that took minutes to decipher. One face mouthed the words that he had been struck by an automobile and was severely injured, but the sounds were muffled and incoherent.

Another face, this one of a young woman, told volumes with the tears erupting from her eyes, but her own lips remained steadfast. He imagined another individual place a piece of clothing, rolled into a thick ball, underneath his head.

Jason's mind was confused with such thoughts, for he felt peace; a kind of spiritual awareness that he had never experienced before. His mind was not anchored by his body, his senses not restricted by the natural.

The faces encircling him seemed to double then quadruple, finally merging into a menagerie of concerned images speaking words that were blocked by an incessant buzzing sound. He looked at them, wondering why they were staring at him. They were speaking, but they didn't allow him the courtesy of understanding them.

One of the faces was replaced by a flashlight that soon blazed its beam into Jason's face. He wanted to shout away the light, but he could not get his mouth to move; no sound seemed to come from his body.

Soon, he seemed to feel a prickling sensation from his upper body that slowly grew in intensity, a series of electrical pulses that tried to force their way upstream against an equally powerful, but less organized counterforce. Jason's mind slowly began to be inundated by more of these sensations, all indicating that something was not quite right, not quite normal.

Almost immediately, Jason began feeling an even stranger sensation, one of his body vibrating profusely, his limbs felt as if they were flailing and functioning beyond his control. As the electrical impulses generated from his body grew in intensity, his mind began to recognize the concept of pain, and the faces seemed to blur, becoming more frosted in appearance.

The images he saw metamorphosed into a strange vision, of a land that he did not recognize, but one that he had felt that he should have known. He saw the sun, or what his mind had assumed to be the sun glowing brightly in a dark sky.

He had the sensation of floating outwards from the sun, passing the recognizable planets that were anything but recognizable as he drew closer. Jason floated past Venus which slowly lost its impenetrable cloud cover as he floated by. He thought that he could see cities beneath the atmosphere with strange vehicles flying around the medium.

Floating past Earth, he maneuvered around space stations of immense size and complexity with apparent shuttle services between the host planet and the artificial structures that seemed to extend forever. He saw the moon approach and dip beneath him, adobe structures lined its surface as far as the eye could see.

Mars appeared within an instant, resembling something of a fractional Earth, rivers flowing across its surface and emptying into a hemispherical sea, bristling with strange vessels that sailed here and there.

Asteroids next appeared, mutilated by industrial processes that his mind could not quite understand, and he observed countless spacesuits crawling around their surface like ants maintaining their hill.

When Jupiter arrived, Jason seemed to float straight towards Europa where he penetrated the surface as easily as he had bridged the gap from the Sun, shooting through literally hundreds of kilometers of ice in seconds, pausing when it reached the liquid ocean below.

He saw the same organic sludge floating on its surface, lapping at the underside of the ice shell, but there was a difference. He saw machines of all kinds darting around in the sludge, extracting portions of it on each pass much like oil skimmers operating within the Gulf of Mexico.

Diving deeper into the sub-Europan ocean, he saw creatures that resembled a cross between small whales and catfish, their feelers searching for food that thrived on the long ice stalactites that hung down into the water from the canopy above. Smaller creatures seemed to clean parasites from the larger ones, flashing brilliant displays of navigational color in the process.

The solar system seemed to fade out as Jason saw a familiar figure in front of him. His beloved Samantha appeared, dressed in a flowing white gown of immaculate embroidery. Although he could see her long hair flowing – the color and length of when they had first met – he could not make out her face. Jason knew it was her, however, by recognizing the wound from the cancer that had eaten away her throat.

He tried to communicate with her, tried to hear what she was saying. He knew that she was telling him something; her lips were moving as she reached up to hug him. Jason desperately wanted to hear her, but the only sound that seemed to surround him was the constant buzzing sound that over time seemed to grew in amplitude and duration.

Soon, the fuzzy tone cleared into a screaming echo as the image of his wife gave way to a trio of faces. They seemed to be wearing masks of some sort, staring down at him and yelling words that he did not know if they were meant for him or not.

The faces fluttered into obscurity and vanished into a brief blackness that turned decidedly white when the fog lifted, giving him the sensation that he was in a room. Unfamiliar faces in teal and purple scurried around him, pushing carts of various sizes before they too disappeared in a curtain of black silence.

EXCRUCIATING PAIN WAS the next sensation that Jason felt, flowing from every corner of his body. His mind was clear, but questioned every sense that flowed into his brain. He looked over to his right side and saw nothing but a white curtain that curled around towards his left.

He continued to stare at the curtain, not quite knowing what to expect of it, until the feeling of a hand distracted his concentration. It was a soft, gentle hand that registered within the grip of his left palm. Slowly and painfully, he allowed his head to fall towards the left, struggling to command his eyes to follow the caring hand up to its owner.

"Don't try to speak." spoke Juanita Wilson, her eyes glistening with tears. "Just lay there quietly."

"You'd better listen to her." added Jack Stephens, who appeared standing behind her. "She's going to be your nurse now, for quite some time."

Jason tried to inquire as to where he was, but could not utter a sound, the rapidly dawning sensation of tubes in his mouth and nose creating a feeling of an artificial, motionless jaw.

"Keep quiet!" barked Jack, reaching around Juanita to pat Jason's hand gently. "You're in a private hospital; you were nailed by a car last month. I flew Ms. Wilson down here to take care of you, seeing how well you two always got along."

"I would've come down myself." added Juanita, caressing Jason's hair. "You're gonna need someone who can *order* you back on your feet." She smiled, but turned away as tears clouded her vision.

Another figure appeared from behind Jack, a beautiful woman with long, fiery red hair. "We're *all* going to get you back on your feet."

"Jamie's right." replied Jack, removing his hand from Jason's side. "We're going to stand by you the whole time until you're well enough to get back to business."

Jason tried to smile, but it was of no use. The tubes blocking his mouth made any movement an exercise in pain, and he feared that he was going to black out at any moment.

He scrutinized the three individuals next to his bed, wondering why they didn't let him die. He missed the vision of Samantha that had appeared to him and an intense feeling of loneliness consumed him. He prayed to himself, *God, why didn't you let me stay with Samantha?*

He turned his gaze towards Juanita who continued to caress his hair; her soft and gentle hands seemed to absorb the pain that flowed through his scalp. He recognized something familiar about her eyes – it was the same caring, devoted sparkle that had appeared within Samantha's eyes during his vision.

He looked at Juanita, slowly remembering his enjoyable days at the Jagged T. He remembered her laughter, her sarcasm, and her caring nature. The tremendous pain that made even breathing unbearable seemed to dissipate slightly as he studied her eyes and recognized the treasure inherent within a beautiful woman's soul.

There must be a reason that God has allowed me to live?

The Saga of The Gatestrian Knights
by
R.J. Godlewski

The Jason Task Series

The Gatestrian Knights
Hazardous Task
The Sea Berets
Kang Zheng
Taliesin

The Migration Series

The Helix Plasma
The Organics of Europa
Jovari
Auxotroph

The Civilization Series

The Cilix Colony
Pibroch
Tantalus 5
Tratestria

The Evolution Series

The Descendants of Maruthe
The Genesinarians
The Sinesas Migration
The Great Novarians
Protocol 454
Epitah of a Planetary System

Printed in the United Kingdom
by Lightning Source UK Ltd.
117555UKS00002B/95

9 781596 820647